D0055943

The Spice Box Letters

Also by Eve Makis

Eat, Drink and Be Married
The Mother-in-Law
Land of the Golden Apple

The Spice Box Letters

Eve Makis

Thomas Dunne Books
St. Martin's Press
New York

THOMAS DUNNE BOOKS.
An imprint of St. Martin's Press.

THE SPICE BOX LETTERS. Copyright © 2015 by Eve Makis. All rights reserved. Printed in the United States of America. For information, address St. Martin's Press, 175 Fifth Avenue, New York, N.Y. 10010.

www.thomasdunnebooks.com
www.stmartins.com

The Library of Congress Cataloging-in-Publication Data
is available upon request.

ISBN 978-1-250-09580-0 (hardcover)
ISBN 978-1-250-09581-7 (e-book)

Our books may be purchased in bulk for promotional, educational, or business use. Please contact your local bookseller or the Macmillan Corporate and Premium Sales Department at 1-800-221-7945, extension 5442, or by e-mail at MacmillanSpecialMarkets@macmillan.com.

First published in Great Britain by Sandstone Press Ltd

First U.S. Edition: September 2016

10 9 8 7 6 5 4 3 2 1

For TM, Emily and George with love

Acknowledgments

I thank the following for their generous emotional and editorial support. Moira Forsyth, my editor, and all at Sandstone Press, the eagle-eyed poet Zoe Piponides, Vartan Tashdjian, Tigran Kalaydjian, Ruth Keshishian, Gabaret Kazandjian, Susan Pattie (Faith in History), Antonia Marcou and The Society of Authors.

Special thanks to my tenacious agent Diana Beaumont for embracing Gabriel Arakelian with such enthusiasm and believing his story needed to be told.

The Spice Box Letters

Chapter 1

Mariam, Eastern Turkey, 1915

Baba drove the carriage at speed, guiding the dapple-grey Arabian through a labyrinth of cobbled streets. The carriage juddered as it struck jagged stones, barbed vibrations stealing up through my backbone. On the street, merchants advertised their wares in a throaty hum or sucked on water pipes in the entrances of open-fronted stores brimming with spices, homespun silks, leather goods, copper pans and aphrodisiacs. There was no hint of danger on the street, no warning of the calamity to come.

The silvery crow of a distant cock rang out over red-tiled rooftops, over domes and minarets and the snow-capped summit that dwarfed the city. Scarfed women in cotton shawls chatted beneath stone lintels. A stray dog suckled her young. The morning air was scented with the ancient odour of incense, burnt sugar and the fruity smoke of shishas. A row of silver charms, inlaid with blue enamel, hung from a doorway; amulets just like the one I always carried in my pocket to protect me from the evil eye.

It felt good to be out of the house, immersed in the hubbub of the market. Our world was a dangerous place, my father warned, and he was not alone in voicing his

1

fears. Dire predictions resounded in every Armenian backyard and coffee house.

The carriage overtook mules transporting kindling and baskets loaded with melons, pumpkins and burgundy figs. Flies hovered at the window of the carriage, straying from the skinny carcass hanging from the butcher's awning. A bell tinkled in the near distance and Baba stopped to let the pastry man cross, his wooden cart laden with diamonds of paklava in gleaming pastry coats.

I shouted over the murmur of the market. 'Baba, stop. I want a pastry.' The salivating scent of syrup and rose water wafted through the carriage.

Baba clicked his tongue, setting the dapple-grey in motion. The pastry seller's rhythmic call of pa-kla-vaaaa faded while a man's angry rhetoric echoed through the street. A crowd had gathered up ahead. People shifted to let the buggy pass into the heart of a drama. The Armenian baker, Kalfayan, stood outside his shop, before the city's Turkish commandant and several police officers, shouting at the top of his voice, his jowly face quivering with rage.

'I've done nothing wrong . . . the allegations are false . . . I did not poison the bread for the barracks.'

The trays in the window of his shop had been upturned and an array of dimpled loaves littered the street.

Kalfayan stepped forward, his hands clenched. The commandant raised his baton and struck him on the temple. Kalfayan's eyes bulged in surprise. A second vicious blow knocked him off his feet and he fell, like an axed tree. I heard his skull crack on the ground, like the crunch of dry eucalyptus pods underfoot. Screams permeated the carriage. The baker lay completely still while the street closed in about him, people flapping like chickens rushing at their feed. I saw my father appear in this scene. My doctor-father down on his knees, taking the baker's pulse, turning his head, his fingers in the baker's mouth dislodging his tongue. Seconds later, Kalfayan spluttered back to life and the police pulled him to his feet. The next thing I knew, the buggy was pulling away, the horse's powerful feet pounding the cobbles.

Chapter 2

Katerina, England, 1985

Mum stands at the fireplace fingering cards that line the mantle, purple poppies, tulips and angels in abundance. *Your mother was a wonderful woman and will be deeply missed.* She reads out other sentiments in the same vein, stock phrases that pluck at heartstrings, words meant to bolster. I watch her face run a gamut of emotions as she pores over more personal messages. *Mariam was a gem, generous to a fault. A wonderful cook who performed culinary alchemy with a shoulder of lamb and smoked paprika.* A nurse for fifty years, Gran had plenty of friends who crammed the church of St Joseph and trailed out of the door. I picture her now, hair silver-streaked, prominent cheekbones, eyes a river green that mirrored my own, shining in her olive-skinned face; inscrutable eyes that impelled a second glance.

I search for words of comfort, wonder how it feels to lose a mother, how long time takes to heal. A month has passed since Gran died and Mum is on a downward slide, her hair lank and unwashed, spirits tethered to the recent past. To say they were close is an understatement. They were more like sisters. I was the third cog in the wheel, joining them for coffee every Tuesday, sharing Sunday lunch at Gran's place where the humble roast

4

was embellished with continental delights, enhanced with garlic, cumin and cinnamon. We were three of a kind, uncannily similar in appearance, cut from the same cloth. At family gatherings we looked like moths dropped into a cluster of cabbage whites. Mum's Asia Minor genes overrode Dad's fair hair and blue eyes when I was conceived.

'I've got something to show you,' Mum says, leading the way upstairs to her bedroom where she lifts a cardboard storage box onto the bed. 'I found this in your grandmother's wardrobe. I thought we could go through it together.'

We sit side by side, resting against the headboard, Gran's treasure trove poised between us. Mum starts delving through a pile of brown envelopes, emptying them of snapshots, mostly of me: cabbage-patch Katerina in Mum's arms; scrawny kid with knobbly knees and pigtails, riding Dad's shoulders; schoolgirl with braces and a gap-tooth grin; graduate in mortar board and vampire cape; Katerina sitting at the news desk of The Echo eating a mid-morning doughnut, poised to write her next story. Katerina *jan,* Gran used to call me, her dearest, love and pain melding in her eyes speaking of everyone she had lost.

One of the envelopes contains a familiar black and white photo scuffed and torn down the middle, a picture of Gran's mother, Gadarine, my namesake. She is lustre-haired and beautiful, wearing a white lace dress with embroidered collar. She was sixteen on her wedding day and in the picture she gazes demurely into the distance. All that remains of the groom is a dismembered hand looped through the arm of his young bride. A copy of the original stood on Gran's mantle, another hangs on the wall of Mum's house. It's the only photo we have of Gran's family, the only tangible evidence of those who came before us. She rarely talked about her kin, as if she had taken a vow of silence, an abstinence of speech that spoke volumes. The only one she mentioned with an irrepressible smile was Gabriel, her brother. She named my mother, Gaby, after him and whenever I sneaked more than my fair share of pudding she used to say, *you're just like Gabriel.*

Mum shuffles through the photos, shaking her head. 'What a shame there isn't a picture of your grandmother on her wedding day. When I was a child, I used to have recurrent dreams about Mum's dress – always the same one, drawn in at the waist with a band of pearl beading.'

Gran said the photographer never turned up on her wedding day and there was no handy friend with a camera on standby.

Mum fishes in the box, pulls out a leather bound notebook and flicks through the yellow-tinged pages.

'I remember seeing Mum write in this book but God only knows what it says. It's all in Armenian.'

She hands over the book and I leaf through an ornamental script, scrawled in fountain pen, navy ink smudged in places, lined sheets thick with lettering that looks like a cross between Greek and Arabic; a phonetic language with an alphabet dating back to AD405, not a single word recognisable.

'We'll have to get it translated. There are dates in here: 1915, 1918. This must be some kind of journal.'

6

'I begged her to teach me her language but she wouldn't. Said there was no point, that learning Armenian wouldn't help me in life. Get it translated, Katerina. I don't care what it costs.'

Mum empties the storage container onto the bed. Inside a length of sackcloth there's a wooden box the size of a toaster, dented at the edges, a scratched painting on the lid. An exotic couple picnic beside a waterfall in a luscious, woody landscape where tropical birds fan their wings. The man wears a turquoise turban and the woman a yellow sari that dips below one of her breasts.

'Looks like a jewellery box. Perhaps it's a love token, Mum.'

'If my father gave it to her, why would she hide it? The picture might have been a bit risqué in its day but it's hardly the Kama Sutra.'

My thoughts turn to Gramps, quintessential English gent, respected local GP, a fan of corduroy trousers and cardigans with leather elbow patches, wearer of half-frame spectacles. He died of pancreatic cancer two years before his wife and left her broken-hearted, a shadow. He was ten years older than Gran and often joked he'd robbed her from the cradle.

'Don't think it was from Gramps.'

'No,' Mum says. 'Exotica weren't his style.'

I click open the tarnished gold clasp and draw up the lid. Airmail envelopes with faded blue and red edging are squashed inside. I spread the contents out on the bed, a dozen sealed envelopes with no name or address. Hesitantly, Mum opens one and pulls out a piece of paper scribbled in Gran's mother tongue and clearly dated 1928.

'Who do you think Gran was writing to?'

'She had one or two Armenian friends but no one who lived abroad, as far as I know. I think the question is why she never sent the letters.'

She opens a second envelope, the letter a page long and dated 1957. I look at Mum, reluctant to voice my thoughts; this hidden stash spanning at least thirty years is the biggest mystery.

'You don't think she was having an affair do you?' Mum doesn't hold back and just the thought makes her eyes water.

She gathers up Gran's belongings, packs them back into the box and slides it towards me. 'You're the journalist. Use your investigative skills. Find out what you can about my mother. Will you do that for me? And please, leave the letters for now; I'm not ready for any nasty surprises.'

I agree to help, relieved the letters are off limits for now. As a child, I thrived on puzzle-solving: crosswords, Rubik's cube, jigsaws, the smaller the pieces, the more I relished the challenge. I would think of Gran's story box as one giant puzzle I would grapple with and ultimately conquer.

'I want to give you something. A keepsake.' Mum opens the drawer of her bedside cabinet and finds Gran's silver pocket watch, a century-old timepiece with a white enamel face and Roman numerals. 'You know how precious it was to her. She would want you to have it.'

I used to spend hours playing with the watch, snapping open the back to inspect the mechanism, wishing it would work. It belonged to Gran's father, Grigor, the key lost in circumstances she refused to talk about. She told us so little about her past, and even less about her girlhood. Occasionally, when nostalgia overwhelmed her, she remembered Gabriel and their antics as children, confessed how much she loved and missed him.

The watch is a tangible connection to the past, a link to Gran's family and her story, my story. It's a seminal moment, sitting on the bed with Mum, surrounded by Gran's hoard that's so much more than a disparate array of objects. I never really understood the fuss people made about antiques: hairpins, snuff pouches and old, decrepit sideboards with sticky drawers. Now, I see that every relic, however battered, every scratch on every knick-knack, is engraved with a timeless story of someone's life.

Chapter 3

Mariam, 1915

A silver arc moon burned outside my bedroom window, softly lighting the volcanic peaks of Mount Erciyes. I lay beside my brother, Gabriel, watching the sky darken over the mountain, wondering what life was like beyond the icy crags. Did other girls lie awake at night gripped by fear and dread? Did sleep bring vivid nightmares that haunted them throughout the day? Was life, on the other side, blighted by war? I asked Gabriel for a story to help me sleep.

'About what? A king, a hero or a werewolf or I can tell you one about an evil angel that wreaks havoc on the world.'

'I don't know. You decide.'

'How about a wedding day story?'

'Is it fun?'

'Not exactly. It's about a man whose wedding didn't go to plan. As he made his way to the altar to marry the woman he loved, the Grim Reaper grabbed him by the throat with vice-like fingers, and said, *hand over your soul.*' My brother assumed the raspy voice of Death, his mouth close to my ear. 'His mother and father offered their souls in exchange but Death refused and then the man's betrothed said, *take me instead.*'

'And did he?'

'Death snatched the woman's soul with one sharp tug as if he were pulling up a radish.'

'And she was gone forever?'

'No. Death began to have regrets. He was impressed by the woman's devotion, her show of love, and so he gave back her soul and the couple got married and the wedding was celebrated for three days and nights.'

I relaxed against the mattress, comforted by the incredible resolution of Gabriel's story. I turned on my side to sleep but as my breathing shallowed, Gabriel whispered hoarsely in my ear, *'Hand over your soul.'* I screamed. He laughed, drew close. 'Sorry I scared you.'

A candle on the bedside cast shadows on the walls, fleet-footed spirits and ghouls with elongated eyes, momentary and malevolent. My fear could see through walls and closets, under the bed; it translated a cat's cry into an unearthly human scream.

Once, I had feared mythical creatures, monsters and spooks. Now I had to contemplate threats that were real: men on horseback, wielding guns and knives, sinking metal into flesh and riding away with human loot.

The Turks had joined forces with the Germans and declared war against France, Great Britain and Russia. Several eastern regions of the Ottoman Empire had already been lost to the Russian army. The Government blamed the Armenians for its defeats, accusing us of siding with the enemy. Armenian communities had come under attack from vigilantes who rode into towns and villages at midnight, torching homes, looting, abducting women and adolescent girls. Mothers had taken to burying their daughters up to the necks, concealing them in hurried mounds until the danger passed.

'What do you think it feels like to die?' I whispered. 'Can you imagine Mother dying? Can you think of anything worse?'

In waking dreams I had often imagined my mother's death, her funeral, the wake conjuring feelings so raw and intense I had wept. The night became a black screen on which morbid scenes jittered like shadow puppets. I wondered if death was like drowning in the darkest shade of black. Gabriel's story played over in my mind, fear spreading its insidious spores.

Chapter 4

Katerina

The following day, I visit Mum and find her in pieces, sniffling over a pan of scorched bulgur wheat. The kitchen's strewn with soiled pots, vegetable peelings, plates piled high in the sink, smoke wisps permeating the house. I sit her down at the kitchen bar, make us both a cup of sweet mint tea just like Gran used to make with a handful of fresh leaves plucked from the garden.

She sniffs, wipes her face with the back of her hand. 'I don't know what came over me. I'm just being ridiculous.'

'What happened?'

'I miss her, Katerina. I miss her so much. Thought I'd comfort myself by making her lamb stew. Wanted to have it ready by the time you came over. I bought all the ingredients, chopped everything up and then realised I didn't know what to do. What spices she used. Cooking times, measurements, nothing. I made it up as I went along but it didn't taste the same and the meat was tough so I turned up the heat and burnt the stew. Then, I tried to make bulgur wheat pilaf, simple enough you'd think, but I ruined that too. I should have written down her recipes while she was still alive, but I never did and now I'll never have the chance.'

13

I miss Gran's cooking too, the particular taste of her concoctions, flavours enhancing my youth, gathering our kin over the years. She never measured anything, never used a timer or consulted a book and never liked anyone meddling in her kitchen.

'You're not being ridiculous. I'd give anything for a taste of her chicken soup.'

'Or a slice of her nutmeg cake.'

'What about that dip she made with aubergines and garlic, though it's not the best thing to eat before a date.'

Mum looks at me hopefully. 'Are things back on with Rob?'

'I wish you'd stop asking.' I should have read the signs but I was too involved, too focused on our rose-tinted future to consider the contradictions. The extravagant gifts, his parents off limits. His declarations of love at odds with his reluctance to share a living space – a history of short relationships. I spared Mum the detail, too proud to admit I'd been taken in.

We recall Gran in her kitchen, bending over sauces, stirring rose-scented syrups with an ancient wooden spoon, finger-thumbing and scattering herbs from a height, relishing the way the sun would spotlight petal flakes as they floated into her bowls. Her cooking was as much our legacy as the photos in the treasure box, an inextricable part of the woman we'd lost and, just like Mum, I wish I'd paid more attention, muscled my way into her kitchen. And then I remember.

'Where's that book I bought you –*Tastes of Home*, I think it was called.'

'On the shelf in the living room.'

I fetch the Armenian recipe book that hasn't been touched in years and search through the index, turn to the page I'm looking for. 'Listen to this. *Lamb stew was traditionally cooked underground in large pits and served with pilaf on feast days. The food was blessed and eaten communally to commemorate the departed.* Let's make some.'

'Sure. I've still got some lamb left.'

We peel, dice and fry, seasoning, tasting, following the recipe to the letter, making a side dish of peppery pilaf with rice and vermicelli. Two hours later, Dad arrives to find a spruced up kitchen and a hot meal simmering in the oven, Mum freshly showered with a powder blush to her cheeks. The three of us sit at the kitchen counter forking pilaf and fall-apart lamb, dolloped with creamy yoghurt, raising glasses of dry red, our spirits lifted. The meal doesn't quite match Gran's gourmet dishes but it's not far off. There seems no better way of celebrating Gran's life, the essence and sparkle of a woman who came alive in the kitchen, more apt than wearing the customary black and mulling over a gravestone.

Chapter 5

On Saturday morning, I'm back at Mum's with a bag of aubergines, a string of fresh chillies and a whole stem of garlic.

'Today's lunch,' I announce, thrusting the ingredients into her arms. 'Baba Ganoush. Page 63.'

She knows the drill, and heads into the kitchen.

For the past week, in the evenings, after work, we've been basting red meat in olive oil and spices, stewing pulses, baking whole fish, rolling meatballs, indulging in cracked wheat salad sprinkled with pomegranate. We've chopped fresh herbs and flavoured our savouries with mint, paprika, tarragon, dill; scented our puddings with vanilla, honey and orange blossom water. I dug out Mum's pestle and mortar and pounded seeds and sticks that filled the house with woody aromas. We've baked diamonds of paklava, as well as rice flour pudding and nutmeg sponge, on a mission to reproduce every dish in Mum's ancestral cookbook.

Mum leafs through the book, reads out the recipe for Baba Ganoush and then we spring into action, skewering aubergines, roasting them on the hob, chopping garlic and a mound of herbs.

'What's happening with the translation?' she asks.

'I've made some calls. I'm waiting to hear back.'

I've done nothing. Every time I think about the journal and letters, my stomach hardens and a sixth sense stops me picking up the phone. Gran hid the contents of that box for a reason. Don't the dead have rights? Am I at liberty to delve into the life she purposely concealed? There's a dark interlude in Gran's life she couldn't share with her family, a stack of letters she never wanted us to see. She died from a stroke aged seventy-six, suddenly, without any telltale signs. Would she have offered up her secrets if she knew how her life would end? I wonder.

We remove the wizened skins of the aubergines, scoop out the sweet flesh, stir in olive oil, seasoning, and chopped chilli. Then we perch at the counter, scooping the appetiser onto triangles of pitta bread.

'Are you alright Katerina, love? You don't look right,' Mum says.

I'm dog-tired, dragging my body through the day but I won't have the spotlight cast on me. 'Work's been full on. Half the newsroom's off with flu.'

'I can tell you're not sleeping.'

I'm likely to give way to tears if she doesn't stop eyeing me in the same way Gran used to – as if she could read my every thought.

'You need a break from all this, Katerina, from work, even from me. Why don't you book that holiday you deserve? I'll still be here when you get back.'

Chapter 6

Larnaca, Cyprus. One month later.

I wake up to the sound of revving mopeds and market traders touting their wares. Across the street, a market is in full swing with stalls selling clusters of vine leaves, horseradish, courgettes, bulging beef tomatoes and hefty bunches of herbs. Rabbits and chickens hang from awnings beside low tables piled high with nuts and dried fruit. The din makes me feel part of the world, even with a hangover.

Bright sunlight sprawls across the room like a recumbent cat, draping a warm paw across my face. Jenny's skinny leg hangs out of the neighbouring bed, drool trailing down her cheek and pooling on her pillow. It's not a snapshot moment for my pretty, blonde friend but it makes her look reassuringly human. Chief sub on *The Echo*, Jenny teeters on the brink of shallow, thinks the cure for losing a grandmother is sun, sea and a bloodstream full of tequila.

I glance at the travel clock on the side table and see we've missed both breakfast and lunch, included in the price of our holiday package. This is no great loss because our hotel is more cheap than cheerful, serving tourist fare, the menu boasting bolognaise and pre-fried nuggets. For three days now, we've been gorging on junk food: greasy sandwiches, burgers and ice cream from American chains that colonise Larnaca's palm tree promenade, a short walk from the hotel. Each day, I wake up intending to root out a cosy corner frequented by the locals and invariably end up in some marble-clad, air-conditioned, soulless outlet, succumbing to familiar dishes, watching the world go by.

Heat steals up through the balls of my feet as I step across the tiled floor to observe the goings-on from the window. Men gather in the local café to drink miniature cups of grainy Greek coffee, thumbing tasseled worry beads. A butcher passes with a goat carcass slung across his shoulder. A gangly old man wheels a heavy cart along the potholed street, pausing outside the hotel, his croaky voice offering a minted yoghurt drink.

Jenny stirs, yawns and stretches her spindly arms. 'Morning, chick,' she says, elbows winging her head. 'Did you sleep well?'

I mumble a disingenuous response because the truth can't be condensed into holiday-friendly blurb. I struggled to sleep, even after half a dozen Mojitos, feeling strangely panicky so far from home.

It's a drizzly March afternoon and a weak-willed sun peers through the loose covering of cloud. Nevertheless, it's a very pleasant 18 degrees. Jenny and I gravitate to our usual haunt and order a club sandwich followed by two scoops of strawberry cheesecake ice cream. The beach across the road is our next port of call where we lie with skirts hiked up and our sunglasses poised, determined, against the odds, to return with a tan. The locals are in jackets and boots while a clutch of sun-starved, North-Europeans relax in gaudy shorts and sunhats.

We're still stretched out on the beach several hours later, no darker in colour but considerably colder and in need of a warming drink. Jenny heads for the Irish pub, decked out in orange pine, a magnet for tourists and expats where English flows as abundantly as the Guinness. I suggest we venture into town, seek out a backstreet joint. We walk along the strip, arm in arm, past hotels, pavement cafés and restaurants, traditional and modern architecture sandwiched together like chipped teeth beside dental veneers. The promenade has an old, stone fort at one end and a colonial customs house at the other, opposite a quaint wooden jetty where local cruise operators offer fishing, diving and sightseeing tours in glass bottomed boats. There's plenty of old world charm in the town, remnants of the island's turbulent past peeking from behind the plastic awnings and neon signs.

On the high street, adjacent to the seafront, we peer through windows and comment on the mix of goods on offer. The usual tourist fodder: shell-clad trinket boxes and armless Venus de Milos immortalised in bronze and plaster. Dusty old shoe shops stand beside glass fronted stores selling designer leather.

We head along a narrow street where the pavements vanish, the shops rundown, and stumble upon an ochre stone building with a heavy wooden door. Several pristine motorbikes pose on the roadside and it's obvious from a glance through the low windows that this stylish bar is where young locals spend their evenings. Jenny heads for the door and I follow, reluctantly, wishing I hadn't led her away from the pub where the dress code is do as you please and the barman greets us with a drink on the house.

My friend swings her hips like a hypnotist's pendulum as she makes her way to the bar and I follow, feeling decidedly out of place. The bar is a world apart from the seaside grunge where Greek Lotharios pick up tourists. The men in this drinking den don't even glance at us, not even Jenny, though the glossy haired, manicured women with matching accessories give us the once over. Reassured by our unkempt appearance, they turn to their drinks and smoke plumes.

We settle at a vacant table in a corner of the bar. A Greek song plays. Not the typical, upbeat, bouzouki riff but a quirkier, haunting male voice and acoustic guitar. For the first time since our arrival I feel we're off the beaten track, tasting authentic island life. Jenny motions towards a man on an adjacent table.

'I won't leave until *he* buys me a drink,' she says.

'One glass and I'm out of here, Jenny. I need an early night.'

Thirty minutes later, the man is firmly rooted at our table. His name's Nico and his friend, who joined us with some reluctance, uttered a name I felt no inclination to hear. Nico and Jenny chat away while I glance awkwardly at the friend whose broody looks are rendered ordinary in the shadow of his perfectly aligned companion. Nico's not only handsome but bright, with a master's degree in business from the London School of Economics. I've been in this unwelcome situation more times than I care to remember, paired up with the less appealing friend. It's time to make my escape.

'I'm going back to the hotel, Jenny. I'm exhausted.'

'No problem,' she replies, eyes fixed on Nico.

He turns to his friend. 'Why don't you give Katerina a lift back to the hotel?'

There's a sharp exchange in Greek, the friend calling Nico a schmuck, I guess, for offering him up as a taxi service but I don't wait around. With a hurried goodbye, I make my way to the door, squeeze through the throng gathered round the bar, struggle to get my bearings on the street outside before heading into a narrow road lined with century-old townhouses. There are no streetlights, no pavement and scant signs of life beyond the age-worn shutters. I hear the low hum of an engine behind me and sense I'm being followed, goose bumps swelling on the back of my neck. A motorbike drives slowly past and comes to a stop a short distance ahead, the rider turning to stare through the dark visor of his helmet. I fumble for the room key in my bag, clutch it in my fist, ready to lash out, cursing Jenny for leaving me to fend for myself. The rider lifts his viser. It's Nico's friend. When he offers m e a lift I quickly accept.

'I didn't catch your name,' he says.

'Katerina. And yours?'

'I'm Ara.'

'That doesn't sound Greek.'

'It's not. I'm Armenian.'

This simple statement sets my mind whirring on the short ride back to the hotel. Fate, and Jenny's penchant for handsome men, has handed me a gift, a key to unlock the secrets of the journal, stored in my handbag along with the watch, to keep a piece of Gran close. Ara pauses outside the hotel and I climb off, wondering how to phrase the question I must ask.

'My grandmother was Armenian.' This confession brings his solemn face to life.' She died recently. I wonder if I could ask you a favour.'

The hotel room is basic. Two narrow beds separated by a scuffed brown table and an uninviting metal chair. We sit side by side on the bed but there's no awkwardness between us. This is a formal arrangement not an invitation for a nightcap. Ara thumbs through Gran's book, eyes widening as he reads short sections aloud in Armenian. He agrees to act as translator and raises no objection to being tagged on my Dictaphone. He tells me the book is a journal of Gran's life beginning in 1915. He begins hesitantly before picking up speed and taking me on a journey to Eastern Turkey where the life of a seven-year-old girl has begun to unravel. He describes a trip in a horse-drawn cart and then preparations which are underway for a neighbour's wedding on the feast day of St Sargis.

Chapter 7

Mariam, 1915

I sat beneath the orange tree with Gabriel, watching my mother, Gadarine, heat sugar and sesame paste in a copper pan. Orange blossom tinged the air, an essence she used to perfume desserts, skin, clothes and hair. Lifting the copper pan by the handles, she carried it into the kitchen and set it down. Lured by the sweet vapour, we followed.

Mama formed small sesame seed piles on the counter, made a hole in the middle of each with her finger, then poured in a spoonful of thick syrup. Plugging the centre with more seeds, she flattened the ball with the palm of her hand, placed a walnut half in the centre, then rolled the mixture around the nut and sliced off each end to make a rectangular confection. She briskly rolled, flattened and sliced until all the ingredients had been used up and dozens of halva cubes were piled neatly onto a painted plate. Mama had spent the morning preparing dishes for a wedding feast later the following day. Esther, the daughter of close friends, was getting married and the usual contributions of neighbourhood hotpots had been arranged well in advance of the celebrations.

I admired Mama's dexterity, her strong, elegant hands that could embroider, plait, knead dough, shape dumplings, polish silver and lather clothes in the stone sink. My mother had been handpicked by her late father-in-law for her beauty and domestic prowess, plucked from her humble village home and transferred to a plush town house in the city of Caesaria. My father was delighted with his bride-to-be, captivated by her pale green eyes and her aura of quiet strength.

Our neighbour, Esther, was the daughter of the town's apothecary, a wealthy and influential man. We had all been looking forward to her wedding for weeks, the dancing and music, a chance to put our worries aside. Gabriel had his mind on the sweets that would furnish the apothecary's table. The wedding coincided with the feast day of St Sargis, the patron saint of youth and love. A day on which girls ate salted biscuits before bedtime to bring on a thirst in the hope future husbands would visit their dreams offering water. The feast of St Sargis marked the start of *Paregentan,* a period of good living and celebration, an extravagant, belly-bloating prelude to Lent and forty days of strict fasting. I loved the rituals of *Paregentan,* the weeks packed with feasting and merriment when presents were given and received. Weddings and baptisms were crammed into these weeks to capitalise on the good will and intensify the festive mood. There was the Feast of Wolves, a day of cleaning and eating to rid the neighbourhood of wild dogs, followed by the mice fiesta when women would put down their darning needles to stop rodents from nibbling their clothes.

Another cause for celebration was the baker's release from prison. His lawyer, Vasag Carabetian, had pulled strings to have him freed, gone as far as sampling the bread the authorities claimed was poisoned, suffering no ill effects. Everyone had heard how my father's prompt action had saved Kalfayan's life after he had swallowed his tongue. Baba was hailed a hero but I was haunted by visions of the baker's head dashed against the cobbles.

Mama offered us a piece of halva, a reward for my patience. The brittle sweet quickly softened to a creamy texture in our mouths. When Mama's back was turned, Gabriel took two more sweets and offered one to me, mischief in his eyes. We ate quietly, laughter contained, swallowed the last sticky mouthful and whined for more but Mama whisked the plate away and ushered us out of the kitchen.

Chapter 8

Katerina

Mid-morning, the following day, I'm lying in bed, churning over Gran's story, wishing I could pick up the phone and talk to her, hear her voice again. She was always there for me, a listening, objective ear through teenage rows with Mum and matters of the heart. She was one of those people with the rare ability to say the right thing, make you see through your blindness, as if she'd seen it all and knew what really mattered. Her advice, offered sparely, had love and compassion at its core.

The phone rings beside the bed. It's Ara calling from reception, saying he wants to take me somewhere. I pull on jeans, leave Jenny a note and make my way to the lift. Ara's outside, perched on his bike. He offers me a helmet and announces we're off to his mother's for Sunday lunch. My protest is drowned by the engine spurring into life. This is Mediterranean hospitality taken too far.

The journey is mercifully short, only minutes from the town centre to a residential area where newly built apartment blocks stand beside shabby bungalows, neighbouring freshly whitewashed villas. Some properties have pitched roofs while others sprout ugly, metal poles, ready for a second floor. Ara pulls up outside a neat terracotta house with a well-tended garden, thick with citrus trees and spindly olives growing in clay pots. There are several cars parked outside and a small, comely woman stands at the gate.

'This is my mother, Arpi,' Ara says, as we approach the gate. 'Mum, this is Katerina.'

Arpi takes my face in her hands and kisses both cheeks, leaving waxy smears of lipstick. 'My son tells me you're Armenian.'

I'm English, I'm tempted to say, raised in an English home with an English father from the Home Counties and a mother brought up in an old mill town at the edge of the Peak district. 'My grandmother was Armenian.'

'Same thing, my dear.' She takes me by the arm and leads me through the hallway into an old-fashioned dining room. An ornate table set with steaming platters is circled by dinner guests: young children, two prune-eyed men and several women. I fight the urge to make my excuses and return to the easy familiarity of my package holiday and a relaxed Sunday lunch of fried calamari with Jenny. A pretty young woman with blue-black hair and full lips responds to my smile with deadpan eyes.

Arpi shows me to the table. 'Everyone. This is Katerina. The young lady Ara told us about.' All eyes turn, bringing a flush to my cheeks. Ara pulls out a seat, sits beside me and, soon, homespun delicacies are being thrust in my direction. I'm introduced to Ara's father, his sister, her husband, their children, family friends and their daughter, Nazeli, the dark haired young woman.

Finally, Arpi lifts up the family's corpulent cat, Apollo, and I shake his paw.

'You OK?' Ara asks.

I nod.

'Taste my mother's lamb stew and you'll be fine,' Ara serves up cubes of meat in a thick sauce that smells heavenly.

I take my first mouthful, the soft lamb melting on my tongue, the peppery sauce pleasantly burning my mouth, taking me back to Gran's kitchen and happy times. It's a moment of pure pleasure and one that amply makes up for my embarrassment. There are more treats to savour. Ara fills my plate with flavours and textures that once graced our Sunday dinner table: vine leaves stuffed with rice and pignoli nuts, garlic-seasoned sausage, deep-fried keofta and aubergine dip. Ara's father pours me a tiny glass of raki and a hush descends as I swallow it down and draw breath to cool my burning throat. Everyone laughs, except for Nazeli who appears to have taken a dislike to me.

People talk to me, converse over me in Greek, English and Armenian. After my second glass of raki, my inhibitions melt away and I chat freely as if I'm in the midst of old friends, enjoying the playful banter, delighted to be experiencing island life from the core.

The children at Arpi's table pay little heed to etiquette, reaching out for second helpings and playing with their food. I promise myself that, if I have children, I won't bind them with rules at the dinner table. The meal is followed by an array of desserts. I'm full to bursting but unable to resist the syrup-drenched paklava that's almost as good as Gran's. Arpi tells me the hundred-year-old recipe has been handed down through generations, an unhappy reminder that my heirloom recipes were lost with Gran. The coffee arrives, thick and sweet, the perfect finale to an exquisite meal.

After dinner, I learn that Cyprus is home to a large Armenian community with its own social clubs, churches, schools and cemeteries. Traditions are upheld and the young are encouraged to marry within the community.

'Tell us about your Armenian family,' Ara's father says, his question throwing me.

'I know very little, unfortunately.'

'Katerina's on a voyage of discovery,' Ara says.

'What was your grandmother's family name?' Arpi asks.

'I've no idea.'

'You don't know your grandmother's family name?' Nazeli's tone is barbed.

'What region of the homeland did she come from?' Arpi asks.

I turn to Ara for help.

'Her grandmother came from somewhere near Mount Erciyes. She could see the mountain from her bedroom window and her father was a doctor.'

Ara's mother looks impressed. 'She must have come from a wealthy family, educated and literate.'

'We'll find out more when we read on,' Ara says. 'Are you ready to dive in, Katerina?'

'Right now?' I wonder if he expects me to share my grandmother's secrets with a roomful of people I hardly know.

'Take Katerina out on the veranda, where you'll have some privacy,' Arpi says.

Nazeli's exasperated huff makes it plain to all that she's far from pleased and it doesn't take a genius to guess why. As I follow Ara, I make a point of lightly touching his arm and feel the rumble of green-eyed monster rearing its ugly head behind me.

Out on the veranda, overlooking a pretty, overgrown garden, fruit trees are studded with citrus blossom. While Ara leafs through the journal, familiarising himself with the story he's about to tell, I ponder his feelings for Nazeli. He showed her no attention over lunch while she hung on his every word and flicked viperous glances at me. He catches me staring and there's a split second exchange, a mutual expression of interest that goes beyond friendly. I reach down to stroke Apollo, his tail winding round my ankles, willing the redness in my cheeks to fade.

Chapter 9

Mariam

I wore my favourite white lace dress with the silk sash and new cream slippers with a fashionable heel. The shoes made me feel sophisticated, older than my seven years. As always, I carried the silver amulet in my pocket, rubbed it between thumb and forefinger, believing in its power to protect me. Mama pulled my hair into a tight plait, secured with a red ribbon, and Baba gave me a feast day gift, a lacquered spice box similar to my mother's, a sign that she would soon teach me the secrets of her kitchen. Inside, there were six compartments, each filled to the rim with different spices: deep red, ochre and leafy green, an array of piquant gems. On the lid a turbaned man shared a picnic with a woman swathed in yellow silk. The couple sat on a brightly coloured rug in a meadow strewn with spring flowers beside a gushing waterfall. I found it exquisite and knew I would treasure it forever.

We headed to the bride's house on foot: my parents, Gabriel and my sixteen-year-old brother, Tovmas. He was tall for his age and had started to mingle with the men folk. We walked along a street inhabited by the city's most affluent: merchants, landowners and scholars educated in France, Belgium and America.

The apothecary lived in a three-storey house, with a wrought iron balcony and heavy wooden door. We arrived to find it open, guests and musicians milling in the wide hallway, admiring the bride and groom. Esther wore a silk dress her mother had taken six months to make. Pearly beading ran the edge of a three-quarter sleeve, a silk corsage was pinned to the bodice; a curl of red hair escaped the matching veil.

The bride walked to the door on the arm of her fiancé, Jivan, her exit blocked by her brother, Diran, a dagger held across his chest. He was a tall, stocky, young man with a thick moustache, quite at ease with the customary weapon.

'You're not coming past me.' He swung the dagger close to Jivan's chin.

'Move aside,' a man shouted. 'Let them out.'

'Pay me first and perhaps I'll change my mind.'

'How much do you want?'

'Whatever you think my sister's worth and then a little more. Times are hard.'

Diran smiled and stroked his palm and laughter rippled through the house. The payment was symbolic, a theatrical ritual I had witnessed many times. Jivan's godfather stepped forward. 'Here's your money. Now, stand aside, Diran, and put that dagger away.'

He handed Diran a bundle of notes and, as the young man stepped aside, the sound of the *zurna* pipe pierced the air. A moment later, the *dhol* player beat his large drum with a stick and the guests, infected by the runaway melody of the *zurna* and the deep thump of the *dhol*, clapped their hands and twisted their shoulders. Noone danced with greater zeal than the apothecary who was delighted that his daughter was marrying into a well-respected family. Only Tovmas was sullen, standing with his arms crossed. He had lost the girl he loved.

Esther's mother, Lousine, sniffled into a handkerchief and the women began to sing a traditional song about the sadness of a daughter leaving home, the melancholic tones picked up by the *zurna* and *dhol*.

The couple began their journey to church on foot, treading on rose petals the women scattered along their path. The wedding party wove through the narrow streets of the city following the musicians. I was carried along by the sea of people and sang along with a group of women whose voices were sweet and inviting. Jivan was the king, the women sang, handsome and strong, and Esther was queen. Jivan was the sun and Esther the moon, a girl blessed with beauty and grace.

The entourage was subdued inside the church of St Gregory. The shadowy interior was lit by candles and bright shafts of light that streamed through stained glass windows. The liturgy began, a harmonious mix of priest, deacon and chorister. The priest switching from subdued murmur to operatic boom and the chorister echoing replies with as much melodic dexterity as the *zurna*. I watched the priest join Esther and Jivan's right hands to symbolise their union, before placing a floral crown on their heads to make them monarchs of their own kingdom. The couple exchanged rings and drank wine from a gold goblet, a symbol of their commitment to share the joys and constraints of life.

The liturgy floated in and out of my consciousness. *Alleluia, Alleluia. Be beautiful and multiply and fill the Earth ... Lord, grant them a peaceful life and lengthen their time in the world.*

Chapter 10

Katerina

Ara's back the next day and asks if I would like to see his workplace. He's in jeans, torn at the knee, olive skin gaping through faded denim, his hair a straw woven nest, auburn hues catching the morning sun. I mount the bike, ignoring the flutter in my chest as I place my hands on his waist. We ride with helmets hinged on our arms, enjoying the luxury of the open air. We pass the bar where we met and turn into a narrow street lined with a variety of workshops, housing a coffee shop, gallery and picture framers. He pauses outside a set of double doors, the panelled wood beautifully restored, held shut by a gleaming, wrought iron latch. There's an alley at the side where he parks by another rustic doorway. He grins expectantly as he holds up an antiquated key. The door creaks open to unveil a charming sculpture garden. Chunky stone carvings are dotted around a yard strewn with potted geraniums, flowered basil and an array of bulbous cacti.

'Welcome to my office,' he says.

'You're a . . . ?'

'Stone junkie.' His hand rests on the small of my back, draws me into his world, its textured, intricate detail.

Close by, there's a six-foot, marble egg and beside it a

waist-height figure with a square nose and flat face, the knees drawn up to the chest. I stroke the grainy surface of the stone.

'What's his story?'

'He's a she, a nude inspired by Cycladic Art: the art of the pagan Greeks. She's a reject. Most of the pieces here are defective in some way but I'm very attached to them.'

We sit at the back of the garden on a quirky limestone bench with a curved backrest and thick, roughly chiselled feet, the smooth rock seat cool against the bare skin of my legs.

'You made this?'

Ara turns, his eyes a warm breath away. 'Do you like it?'

'It's sort of Gaudi meets the Flintstones.'

'Not exactly a straight answer.'

'I write for a living and try to avoid clichés as a matter of principle.'

'And to say you love something is cliché?'

'The word's overused, bandied around, most people don't know what love means.'

There's a bitterness to my tone I can't help and his face darkens but he doesn't pry and, even if he did, I wouldn't admit the reason for my cynicism. My romantic disappointments are not a topic for casual conversation between acquaintances. I remind myself that when Ara's task is complete, I'll find him an artistic gift as a token of appreciation and we'll part with a handshake, return to our respective lives, 2,000 miles apart. I reach for Gran's journal in my bag and he takes the hint, strategically shifting his body away from me. The opening lines thrust us back into the heart of a wedding celebration where guests are spilling out of a church into bright sunlight, making their way to the groom's house for a festive gathering.

Chapter 11

Mariam

Esther was greeted at the door of her new home with gifts, before the men slunk away to drink raki and tease one another with humorous chants. Platters of food were laid on a long table in the back yard. Roast lamb stuffed with cracked wheat and spices, soft flatbread, creamy yoghurt in clay pots. Cabbage leaves stuffed with rice and meat. *Patila*, layered pastry squares, spread with cheese and butter. My mother had cooked her talked-about *kuluk*, sheep's head stew, and several desserts, including halva and *pkhpkhig*, sweet dough balls, deep fried and drizzled with honey. Paklava had been delivered earlier that day by the Turkish pastry man and sat beside a plate of salted biscuits.

Guests poured through the open front door, commenting on the wonderful aromas. I sat in the shade of a pear tree with Gabriel, munching sweets. Friends and relations formed small clusters or reclined on soft cushions while the musicians rested on their haunches sipping tea. Our neighbour Nvart was spreading gossip about other people's children while scanning eligible youths suitable for her daughters. My father stood with a group of men who were gathered around the lawyer, Carabetian. Baba wore a black suit with a tailed jacket, a silver pocket watch hanging from the buttonhole of his waistcoat, the timepiece bought in Geneva on the day of his graduation. He was the first doctor in the Arakelian family and determined not to be the last.

There is nothing nobler than saving life, he liked to say, nothing more rewarding than alleviating human suffering. His intuitive mind craved the intellectual challenges his profession demanded. He often worked through the night on medical riddles, on symptoms he struggled to diagnose by day, consulting his library of books until answers came to him. Baba's passion for his work was contagious and I was infected early on, leafing through the medical documents he left lying around.

He was respected in the city, treating both Turks and Armenians, waving his fee for poorer folk. People clustered around him in the street, hung on his every word. No part of his life was out of bounds, no time of day or venue sacrosanct. He went to church or sat in a coffee house while the sick and neurotic drifted towards him, clutching their abdomens, complaining of sore throats and belly aches, expecting an immediate cure.

Carabetian's voice carried across the yard.

'The men are discussing politics again,' Gabriel said. 'I'm sick of hearing about it.'

'The world's at war, Mariam. Do you expect them to discuss the price of melons?'

We tuned into the angry rhetoric.

'The situation is getting worse by the day. The nationalist factions are gaining support in the government and we have no friends among them.'

Carabetian was the most outspoken of the men,

most critical of the Ottoman government, most actively involved in the fight for Armenian rights. He was highly respected, had Turkish friends in high places and had appealed directly to members of the government's liberal wing for reform. In court, Carabetian represented Armenian clients with grievances against the state, whose land and property had been seized illegally, whose word was secondary to that of a Muslim with his hand on the Qur'an.

'The law can't protect us,' Carabetian said. 'Only a gun can do that. Friends, I urge you all to keep a loaded rifle for any eventuality.'

'But the government has ordered us to surrender our weapons,' Nvart's husband, Mihran, said.

Carabetian snorted. 'Why do you think they want our weapons?'

'For the war effort.'

'To disarm us.'

'But keeping a weapon is punishable by death. '

'Whole battalions of Armenian soldiers, conscripted into the Turkish army, have been shot. Being unarmed is a death sentence.'

Baba turned to Mihran. 'If the government told you to jump off a cliff would you do that too?'

'The Ottomans say we're in league with the enemy, that we're planning an uprising in Istanbul to clear the way for the allies,' Carabetian said.

Mihran sighed. 'Isn't that what we all want? The cavalry to come and save us, protect us from whatever the Ottomans have in store.'

'If it were possible, yes, but there aren't enough of us.

This is all about land, driving us out, recovering territory lost to the Russians in previous wars.'

For a while the men fell silent, lost in thought, sipping raki.

'We have to protect ourselves and take up arms if necessary,' Carabetian said.

Mihran sucked air through his teeth. 'You're a scaremonger. Cynical to the bone. Any hint of real trouble and the nations of Europe will rush to our aid.'

'Right now, the Europeans have more pressing matters to think about.'

'Come on, Carabetian. Lighten up. The authorities have no intention of pursuing us. We're all useful to them in some way. Doctor Grigor in particular. They'll need him to tend to their wounded soldiers. He's far too valuable a commodity to squander.'

This was the most heartening opinion I had heard in weeks and it gave me hope that my father was protected by his profession. Baba turned to his friend, the poet Samuel Badalian, and asked for a ballad. Badalian began a solemn performance, his voice mellifluous. His poem was allegorical, alluding to a series of events in our turbulent history, to uprisings and massacres in the not-so-distant past. Badalian's verse fired his audience and one by one the men expressed their fears for the future.

Baba, Carabetian and the poet Badalian knew their station as leaders of their community. They felt themselves so powerfully rooted in the world, so essential, they believed nothing, not even the might of the Ottoman Empire, could eradicate them. Their impassioned debates made them feel so alive they never thought about death. They had so much to say, to contribute, to think, to thrash out amongst themselves, they believed God would grant them time. They often talked into the night without reserve, without considering that their passionate voices filtered into the street.

The conversation had me on edge and, when someone dropped a plateclose by, I almost jumped out of my skin. Esther's mother rushed over to the broken fragments with a broom and began to sweep up. My mother took the broom from her hands, turned it over, patting the bristles, picking off fluff.

''That's no way to treat a bride,' she said.

'Cover her modesty,' Gabriel shouted and everyone chuckled.

Esther's mother took off her thin shawl and tied it round the brush. Mama turned the broom this way and that and sang a love song in a sweet voice that silenced Carabetian and brought a smile to Baba's lips. Other women joined in and the musicians plucked up the pace. Gyrating hips gathered around the broomstick bride. The women twirled and twisted, snaking their hands, while the men crouched low and leapt, clicking their fingers. Baba reeled on one foot and clapped his hands. Esther danced close to Jivan, hands on hips, her gaze lowered, cheeks flushed. Gabriel took me by the hands and we danced, twirling round and round the broomstick until we grew breathless and the world began to spin.

Angry shouts stilled me. Mama's singing petered out. Half a dozen Turkish policemen stormed the gathering,

Carabetian tailing them with irate calls. I gripped my brother's hand, body tensing.

'What's going on?' I whispered.

'They've come to make arrests.'

News filtered from the hub – the Turks had come to take away the groom, his father-in-law, Mihran and Carabetian. The lawyer would not have it. He blasted insults at the officers until he was shoved to one side and fell against the table. Food scattered at our feet, rolled in the dust, patila, paklava and Mama's carefully-moulded halva. Baba raised his hands to still Carabetian and the men were led away, my father joining the line of captives.

'Gabriel. Where's Baba going?' I asked.

The eyes he turned to me were full of anger. 'They've arrested Baba too.'

Mama's face, filled out by pregnancy, was blanched with fear. I rooted through my pocket for the lucky charm but it was gone, lost while I was dancing and I knew this was an ill omen.

We spent the rest of the day in church, kneeling before the altar with Esther and her mother, Jivan's kin and neighbours who had come to show their support. The women rocked back and forth pleading with God to save their husbands and brothers. Their murmurs filled the church, their repetitious prayers growing louder in my ears. In this church with its gilded altars and pictures of St Gregory holding a flaming cross, I had always felt the presence of God. Spellbound by the choir, I believed in angels and heaven. When the priest sang mass in our ancient tongue and the choir retorted in exultant, melancholic tones, my spirit dipped and soared.But that day, the church was a cold, empty place. I knew our prayers would not be answered, that Death could truly visit a man on the day of his wedding.

The following day Baba was accused of planning a violent rebellion against the Turkish authorities. When a loaded rifle was discovered beneath our floorboards, father's fate was sealed. No amount of bribe money could secure his release. Carabetian faced similar charges and was the first to be tortured and dispensed with. He was hanged upside down, the bottoms of his feet sliced off, his raw flesh ladled with salt. Failing to secure a confession, his torturers pulled out his toenails with pliers and left him suspended, blood pooling in his brain. Jivan and his father-in-law were removed from the prison at night and never returned. The bridal suit and wedding ring were sent back to Esther along with my father's pocket watch. Only Mihran managed to escape and remained in hiding. I hoped that my father would be spared, that his work would save him.

On a bright spring morning, five days after the arrests, Mama left the house, dressed in black, telling us to stay indoors. I sat on the floor hugging my knees. Gabriel paced the room. Tovmas drummed his head with his fists before charging out. Gabriel and I followed him along the street, struggling to keep up.

Before long, we reached the main square where a noisy crowd was assembling and women were weeping before three newly constructed gallows.

I stood on a stone wall and saw the arrival of a

horse-drawn cart. Three hooded men sat in the wagon with their hands tied behind their backs. The first of these men was led to the gallows. He showed no resistance, made no sound, walked with his back arched. When the hood was pulled off his head, it took a while for me to recognise my father. He was pale and dishevelled, bruised below his right eye. I began to shout, screaming out for Baba. His eyes searched the crowd and locked onto mine, telling me to be strong, speaking of his deep love. I watched the noose being slipped over his head and a second later the ground disappeared beneath his feet. I heard my mother's screams mingling with my own, and then I passed out.

★★★

Ara closes the journal and looks at me, gauging my reaction. I am deeply affected, on the edge of tears and glad of the arm that circles my shoulders. I should have known what Gran had to live through, what her young eyes were forced to witness and her mind could never erase. The nightmare doesn't end here, instinct tells me, but what could be worse than seeing your father hang? My mind returns to the spice box, a feast day gift from my great-grandfather. Why was it hidden in the depths of Gran's wardrobe? Why not displayed with pride? Perhaps it stirred too many memories and reminded her of the day she saw her father take his last breath.

Chapter 12

The next day I make my way to Ara's workshop, a take-away frappé in each hand, and find him scrutinising the oval hunk of marble, crosshatching marks with a chisel and steel-headed hammer, his hair flecked with stone dust. He's engrossed, right hand hammering rhythmically, left steering the chisel over the grooved surface. He stands back to take a look just as my foot crunches down on a stray lump of plaster.

'Hey! I wasn't expecting you.' He rubs his hair self-consciously, white specks filling the air as he steps towards me, grinning. 'Sorry ... I look a mess.' He embraces me the Cypriot way and places a light kiss on each cheek.

'I'm not disturbing you, am I?'

'No. Not at all. It's good to see you and I could do with a break.' For a moment, his eyes scan me head to toe, gallantly resting on my hands that are as flushed as my face. 'You've brought the journal?'

'And coffee.' I make for the stone bench, take in the contours of the giant egg stone that looks like a hunched figure but could evolve into two. 'What's that you're working on?'

'Friendship. A copy of a bronze statue below the

47

Canterra Tower in Canada, commissioned by a man who recently lost his wife. It was a favourite of hers and, now she's gone, it will be his little Taj Mahal for the back garden.'

'Nice way to be remembered.' So much better than slabs of stone, lined up like dreary dominoes.

'Do you want to have a go?' he asks. Before I can muster a response, he pulls me up and hands me the hammer and chisel. He fetches tools for himself and shows me exactly what to do, tapping the chisel head with a two-pound hammer to form a shallow ridge. He nods encouragingly as I gingerly etch my own, indelible, mark into the stone, before tapping away with greater confidence, finding a new sense of pleasure in the sound of hammering in stereo, rubbing shoulders with Ara, feeling his breath, like the warm waft of cinnamon bark.

Chapter 13

Mariam

A cool breeze blew through the bathroom window and rippled my hair. Mama stood behind me, scissors in hand, poised and sighing. She began to snip. Dark strands formed soft hillocks around us. I had always worn my hair long, loving the way it shone when Mama brushed it, the way it fanned out when I twirled to the sound of her singing. I whiled away time twisting strands, pulling plaits, making flower-garlands. I loved my long hair but I didn't cry when Mama cut it off. We were all dried out after Baba's execution the previous month.

When Mama had finished, she told me to wear one of Gabriel's suits. I would be safer travelling as a boy. She left the room and a shiver pinched the back of my neck, the weight of a phantom plait pressing against my back. I stared impassively into my father's shaving mirror, seeing a bald child with hollow eyes and a thin face. Raising a hand to my head, I tried to familiarise myself with the stranger.

I heard Gabriel's heavy footsteps on the stairs. He came into the bathroom hiding his shock behind a smile.

'You have a nice round head,' he said. 'Mine's as flat as bread. He ran his hand along the top of his crown, the butt of jokes among our friends.

'Everyone will laugh.'

'Noone laughs anymore, Mariam.'

'What would Baba think if he could see me?'

'He'd be proud of you. I'm proud and a little jealous. You're a better looking boy than me.'

Later that morning, I sat with Gabriel on our front step. The word *sopkiet*, exile, was daubed in black paint on the wall of our house and signalled our expulsion from the city. The quiet neighbourhood had turned into a noisy bazaar. Shouts rang out and the wheels of horse-drawn carts ground up the dry earth. Overloaded donkeys brayed their objections and people haggled, hurriedly selling their possessions before the order to move out echoed through the street and the exodus began. Tovmas took whatever money he was offered for our goods: rugs, clothes, medical books, paintings, furniture. I watched a man stuff his arms into an old jacket of my father's, pulling it tight around his fleshy waist. Tovmas took the man's money and threw him a venomous look.

Many came that morning to cash in on our misfortune, others came to say goodbye. Turkish neighbours provided bread. They kissed Mama and wept. Our carriage and grey horse had been taken by the authorities and we had been given a donkey in exchange. My mother, five months pregnant and dressed in widow's black, loaded up rugs and blankets, and leavened bread, baked hard to last.

Where was God, I asked myself. Why had He taken my father when we needed him most? Why was He allowing people to be herded like cattle, plucked from their homes and marched to camps in the Syrian desert? The government had passed laws sanctioning our deportation and the immediate confiscation of our property. We were backstabbers, in league with the enemy, a threat to the nation's security.

People moved with a sense of urgency, packing bags, feeding babies, sewing children and money into their clothes. My father's heirlooms were scattered on the roadside: armoires, closets, a gilt-edged mirror, a four-poster bed. We had to leave behind so many cherished belongings: Baba's books, my white lace dress, the wooden box still filled with spices that would never be used.

Gabriel carried two photographs and we pored over them; one had been taken on our parents' wedding day. Mama looked so young and Baba's eyes were so powerful and penetrating it was hard to believe he was dead. In recurrent nightmares, I relived his death, waking up in a shivery sweat. Then other worries came to mind. Who would care for his grave when we were gone? Who would pull up the weeds and tend the flowers? Who would drink spirits over the tombstone on memorials?

In the other, more recent photograph, I was pictured in lace and ribbons while my brothers wore suits, hair oiled and swept back, shoes as shiny as beetle wings. There was real excitement on the day the photographer came, neighbours and friends gathering in the yard to watch and take their turn to immortalise their own families. The photo was a painful reminder of a life I had taken for granted.

Mama took the picture from my hand and slipped it in her pocket.

'Let me carry the other picture, Gabriel,' I asked.

As the call to move out rang through the street he tore the picture in half.

'You take Mama,' he said. 'I want to keep Baba close.'

'Stay with your sister, Gabriel,' Mama said, leading the way with Tovmas, pulling the donkey behind her. Gabriel took my hand and I sensed his resolve to be my guardian.

Chapter 14

Katerina

I arrange to meet Ara the following afternoon. He's as keen as I am to continue the translation, though part of me wishes the journal had never been found. I dab some colour on my lips, take greater care with my appearance than I normally would for a casual meeting, Thankfully, Jenny has a friend to occupy her time while I explore the mysteries of the journal, ponder over loose ends.Gran's spice box, for one, left behind when she was forced out of her home but later, inexplicably, back in her possession.

On the road outside, Ara is sitting on his bike, the sun catching his face, reflected in his eyes.'Let's go somewhere quiet,' he says and this excursion feels unnervingly like a first date.

'Where d'you have in mind?'

'The Troodos Mountains.'

We ride out of town, past a stone aqueduct that leads to a motorway cut through a hilly landscape. My arms are wrapped around Ara, quite at ease, no longer the novice on his bike; I tighten my hold, sandwich my body to his as we join the dual carriageway and overtake a lorry loaded with unsuspecting sheep headed for the abattoir. I fight the childlike urge to shout *are we there yet?* over the din. I'm mildly relieved when Ara pulls off the motorway but fear sets in when we begin our ascent, through the heart of small villages. The road narrows and the air thins as we wind our way up the mountainside past conifers, yarrow and thyme bushes, shadowed by spiralling clusters of pine, cedar and fir trees. The altitude numbs my ears and the ramps and hairpin bends set my pulse racing. On one side of the road looms the craggy, pine-strewn face of the Troodos summit and on the other lies a sheer drop that makes me feel distinctly queasy. I rest my head on Ara's back and angle my face upwards, seeking release in an azure sky, praying we don't plummet into the rocky ravine.

I sigh with relief as Ara stops the bike in a lay-by where we cup our hands and drink from a fresh water spring. Only then do I inhale at length, enveloped by the languorous, woody scent of Troodos pine. A picture-postcard village cleaves to the mountainside, white-washed cottages with red-tiled rooftops cluster around a Byzantine church; a vineyard cascades down the steep hill above us, while sweet spring water trickles down the rock face.

An old man in black pantaloons approaches on a donkey, his bristly moustache stretching beyond his smile. He thinks nothing of negotiating the steep roads and riding four-legged alongside the precipice. He stops to offers figs from the basket on his saddle, ripe green bulbs that ooze purple honey when we prise them apart. The old man's face is kindly, his eyes bright and alert. He chats to Ara before splashing his hands and face, swallowing in noisy gulps at the spring.

On the bike, I tell myself to be brave, like the weathered old man. I'm swept up by the beauty of pine-clad hills, village architecture and roadside chapels, the air crisp and fresh.

Ara pulls off the main road and rides along a narrow rutted path bounded by ferns before coming to a stop on the fringe of an orchard. We wade through a grove of fruit trees in bloom, a gentle breeze unsettling a hail of pink and white blossom.

'Do you like it here?' he asks.

There's nothing to spoil the vista, no buildings or telephone wires, no road signs or fences, just acres of luscious green and a mountain spanning the horizon. 'It's breathtaking.'

'Then you won't mind returning to help with the picking.'

'This place belongs to you?'

'My grandfather left it to me in his will. We used to come here together every weekend when I was young, just the two of us. When I'm in the orchard I feel he's not so far away. I want to build a house up here one day, plant more trees, grow vegetables, live off the land. My family think I'm crazy and so do my friends.'

'Who are you going to live up here with? Nazeli?' The thought spills into the open, unadulterated.

He splutters a laugh. 'Nazeli likes her creature comforts. Her cafés, designer labels and shoe shops.' He pauses, searches my eyes. 'There's nothing going on between us, you know. Not anymore.'

'But there was?'

'Our parents go back a long way. We grew up together.

In a perfect world we'd be married with three kids and everyone would be happy. We dated for a while but it didn't work out. We want very different things in life.'

He opens up, telling me about his life while I am sparing with the details of mine. I discover Ara was sent to an English school in Cyprus, the fees paid by his grandfather, and then studied fine art in Manchester before returning to the island where he set up his workshop and moved into a flat in town.

'So you like it up here.' he says, pensively, his eyes resting on mine. 'Could you live somewhere like this, Katerina?' The sound of my name lingers and sensing his thoughts I instinctively grasp at a cool-headed response.

'I'd like a place to escape to but I wouldn't want to live too far away from my friends and family.'

He is stumped for a second but then his reply is unequivocal. 'I couldn't live in England. Three years in the North were enough for me. I can't stand the weather.' The memory ruffles his brow and, in the moment of silence that settles, an unbridgeable gulf forms between us. Ara's looking for a soul mate, an earthy girl who can share his passion for the mountains, and I have ruled myself out of the running.

We take a stroll through the orchard and pick blossom and munch on stalks of wild asparagus and tiny berries, our exchanges clouded by polite formality. The underlying tension grows till Ara pauses at the base of a cherry tree.

'Katerina,' he whispers my name, taking hold of my hand and our eyes meet full focus. 'Time for the journal?' he says.

Chapter 15

Mariam

We joined the masses streaming out of the city, like ants hosed out of their nests. Some of the women wore smart European jackets and long skirts, others were dressed in crumpled smocks and had scarves tied around their shoulders and heads. I was not alone in donning a guise. Many girls had had their faces daubed with earth and coal to mask their good looks. A line of Turkish soldiers walked alongside us, lashing out with their batons, hitting donkey hide or the head of a laggard. Screams and the pounding of doors was our soundtrack out of the city. Those who refused or were unable to leave were dragged out of their houses. I stared into empty homes through gaping doors, shattered shutters. Walls had been torn down and floorboards hacked in an effort by the authorities to find Armenian guns and ammunition, to root out any signs of resistance.

We travelled as a group with Lousine, Esther, Nvart and her two daughters. Out in the countryside, we stayed close together, sharing food and water, sleeping communally in simple tents made from cotton sheets. We were all especially kind to Esther, whose loss seemed the greatest, a husband and a father, a brother under arrest. It seemed God had closed his ears to the priest's blessing on the day of her wedding. Esther's wedding ring hung from a chain around her neck.

Most of the time, Esther walked with Tovmas who seemed to have forged a way through her misery. Behind them, I listened to Tovmas tell Esther we were headed for America where a robed colossus would greet us. His descriptions of the place were so vivid I thought I could hear the waves lashing the side of the vessel that would carry us to safety and a new life, where we would smell the salt air of New York harbour.

Tovmas had morphed into our father. The spirit of Grigor had entered his body, filled his pores, shaped his contours, taken his voice. Whenever I saw Esther smile at Tovmas, I dared to believe in happy endings. Esther and Tovmas falling in love, getting married, having a son who looked just like my father. I dared to hope that life would right itself, that our luck would turn when we reached the shores of America and I would recover from the shock of witnessing my father's final moment.

As the days went by, food began to run out. The sick and elderly struggled to keep up. Mothers groaned beneath the weight of the smallest child hunching their backs. Water was scarce and the sun grew hotter by the day, burning our faces, the backs of our necks. Mama tried to bolster everyone's spirits by singing as we walked but, as the days turned to weeks, misery spread like contagion. The first dead body stopped me in my tracks, making me retch. It was the corpse of a baby girl, naked and wasted, lying in a ditch, facing the heavens. Mama covered my eyes but not before I had taken in all the details. Mottled, inky skin and rotting, pinhole eyes. Thread-like limbs.

The next day, I was still thinking about the baby, imagining vultures peeling off flesh. A Kurdish horseman approached the convoy on a sinewy animal, his face swathed in chequered cloth. I watched him ride along the scraggy line of exiles, sword aloft, ordering young girls to show him their faces. As he came closer, Mama warned me to turn my face to the ground but I watched, fearful and curious.

The horseman tugged off Esther's headscarf, setting her red curls free. He swooped down, grabbed her by the hair and slung her over his horse like a bag of grain. She struggled, screamed, clawed at the man's face but he held on tight and lashed her with his whip. Lousine pleaded for mercy, and then Tovmas rushed at the horseman, grabbing him by the leg. A firm kick knocked him to the ground and the horseman galloped away with Esther still screaming, struggling to free herself, calling for her mother. Lousine sank to her knees and sobbed, refusing to stir even when a guard nudged her with his rifle and ordered her to walk. Mama tried to pull her to her feet but she refused to budge. We left her there and walked on, looking over our shoulders until Lousine disappeared from view and her terrible cries faded.

Chapter 16

Mariam

As darkness fell we set up camp, built fires, ate what little food we could scavenge. I settled down for the night beside Gabriel and tried to sleep but shouts and screams rang out, keeping me awake. We lay on hard ground, solid and rutted. I tried to conjure my father's image but his face had already started to fade.

I reached for Gabriel's hand, voice quivering. 'I miss Baba.'

Gabriel squeezed my fingers. 'He hasn't left us, Mariam. He's travelling with us. Protecting us.'

'How do you know?'

'We're still alive, aren't we?'

'All I feel is his absence.'

'Why don't I tell you a story to help you sleep: about a beautiful girl with long dark hair who went to fill a gourd with water from the river. There, she saw a handsome youth lying on the riverbank and instantly fell in love. The couple kissed and promised themselves to one another but their parents wouldn't allow them to marry.'

'Why?'

'He was a goat herder and she was the daughter of the town's richest man. Her mother, a mean, manipulative woman, sent her away to a distant land to keep her from the boy. Years later, the girl returned to the river where she found the youth, lying just where she had left him, his skin shimmering. When he saw her, he rose into the sky with a flourish of seraphic wings and then, all of a sudden, he fell to earth and died. The girl's heart broke and she died too and the couple were buried together, becoming stars and ascending to heaven. Overcome with grief, the youth's five brothers passed away. One by one they rose into a sky as dark as henna paste where they glimmered like fireflies for all eternity.'

'Why did you tell me such a sad story?'

'The ending was happy.'

'They died of broken hearts!'

'You can't die of a broken heart, Mariam, and anyway, they were reunited in heaven which means, one day, we'll see our father again.'

It was a comforting thought and I closed my eyes and tried to sleep. As I drifted off, a woman began to scream in the near distance, pleading for her life. It was too dark to see but I heard the gallop of hooves, a horse snorting. The woman's shouts faded but the sound of a girl sobbing continued into the night. Another woman had been taken and would disappear into the ether as if she had never existed.

'I can see them,' Gabriel said.

'See who?'

'The Seven Stars. There they are. Right above us.'

My mind was on the woman who had been captured and the sky was nothing but a ceiling of black.

'Let's pretend we're alone,' Gabriel said. 'Pretend we've just had a picnic, that our stomachs are full of sarmas and oranges and Mama's delicious halva. Imagine we're lying down after our feast, bellies fit to burst. Stare up at the sky, Mariam, and forget everything else. It's the only way of escaping this place.'

I stared more intently at the sky, trying to shut out the sounds that grappled with my consciousness. After a while, I began to lose myself, to feel weightless, forget where I was, conscious only of the sky and Gabriel's warm body pressed against mine. The longer I stared, the nearer and brighter the stars appeared. The endless sky was the only world that existed. I left the hard patch of ground and became a reflection of a star, a tiny but vital part of the Cosmos. Slowly, the speckles of white light took on a new guise. Embedded in the darkness were a boy and a girl and five brothers celebrating their reunion in a world beyond sight, a family granted immortality, the energy of their souls burning eternally. As the dense gauze of black began to unravel and the stars paled, lighted coals grown ashen, I fell into a deep sleep. For the first time since his death, my father came to me in a dream, telling me to be strong, offering water and bread.

When I opened my eyes, I saw my mother holding a girl in her arms. 'This is Alitz Tavlian. She will be travelling with us,' she said. 'If anyone asks, say she's your sister. Poor Alitz lost her mother last night.'

The girl flinched, her red eyes swelling. I wondered how it would feel to lose my own mother, to find myself alone with my brothers. It was the worst thing I could imagine and made me breathless with worry.

We were driven on across dusty swathes of land, over hills where nothing grew. Rocks and thistles scarred our feet and an unforgiving sun blistered our cheeks. The guards bypassed towns and villages to keep us out of sight. We survived on mouthfuls of dry bread, occasional sips of water, on roots and bulbs dug from the ground. We joined caravans expelled from other regions, people who looked like the living dead forced to wander the Earth as penance.

I had grown used to the filth, the stench of unwashed skin. Lice infested my clothes, the matted tufts of my hair. I scratched constantly, making my scalp bleed and crust. I had stopped asking my mother for food and tried to ignore the hunger pains that twisted my gut and made me gasp.

The dead baby was the first of many corpses that tainted the air with the acrid smell of death. Everyday someone in the convoy collapsed on the drive east, from sickness, fatigue and starvation. Those too weak to walk were left to rot, stripped of their clothes and jewellery by Kurds who descended from the surrounding hills at night, vultures feeding on human carrion.

Relations in the group had grown cold, Mama distancing herself from Nvart and her daughters. Nvart had stopped sharing food, saving whatever she could beg or scavenge for herself and her children. Other resentments bubbled to the surface. How had Nvart's husband escaped from custody? Why only him? Mama suspected he had collaborated with the authorities, saving himself by betraying his friends.

One month into the journey an ox-cart approached

the convoy with two rifle-toting guards slumped in the wagon. An announcement was made that twenty boys between the ages of six and sixteen would be driven to a local school and given food and fresh clothing before rejoining their families. It was the first time in weeks I had seen my mother smile and she was the first to dash forward and offer the driver money to take all three of us.

'Please take my boys,' she said. 'They need to eat or they will die.'

The driver pocketed the notes she pulled from the hem of her dress.

'Thank God I had the foresight to dress you as a boy,' she whispered.

I wanted to stay and clung to my mother but she lifted me into Tovmas' arms with the words: *this is your chance to live, Mariam.*

Boys clambered onto the wagon, most too tired and hungry to express emotion. As the cart pulled away, I watched the blurred images of my mother and Alitz disappear from view, Mama's scent carried on my palms. Tovmas pulled us close and, in the hollow formed by our bodies, he opened his hand to reveal our father's silver pocket watch, inscribed with his name, a treasure kept hidden from the guards. We kissed the watch as if it were an effigy of Baba and felt his spirit travel with us.

We were driven two kilometres away, out of sight and earshot, through dense forest and out again. The cart came to a stop in a clearing and we were told to climb down. We huddled together, glancing around. There was no schoolhouse, no food or clothes to be seen. A songbird trilled for a mate, the singing at odds with the cold fear that wrapped me in a dank shroud. While the driver looked on impassively, the guards moved closer, began circling us, and then, without warning, they lashed out with their bayonets, stabbing and slashing, cutting into flesh while startled swallows rose from the trees, their wings fluttering.

Some boys were taken by surprise and fell silently; others tried to run away. They were pulled back by the hair, their throats slit. The assault on Tovmas was quick. I watched a bayonet being pushed through my brother's ribs, saw him fall and crumple, heard his dying groan. Gabriel pulled me by the hand but I was paralysed by fear, rooted to the spot. I saw the point of a bayonet slicing his face and a second later the same rod of cold steel, glazed in my brother's simmering blood, was pushed through my abdomen penetrating flesh and sinew, brushing passed bone, twisting, retracting. I fell. Played dead.

Within minutes the screaming subsided and quiet returned to the clearing, but for birdsong and the panting of the guards, whose veins pulsed with intent. Dragging limp arms and legs, they tossed us onto a pile, like mangy carcasses, before climbing aboard the cart.

Blood seeped through raggedy clothes, oozed and dripped, sapping the dying of the life force that had surged through their bodies moments earlier. Soaked up by the earth, the blood darkened and congealed. The children lay tangled around me, their heads thrown back and their mouths agape or horribly twisted, terror cemented on their faces.

I gulped in air from beneath this human stack, my clenched fingers unfurled and I clawed the ground, struggling to free myself, and then I screamed, releasing a cry filled with anguish and horror. I crawled on hands and knees to a patch of clear ground where I sat rocking and crying until another corpse came back to life and dragged its way towards me, a boy called Levon who was caked in dirt and blood, a subhuman being, eyes spilling with fear.

Tasting death, we limped back to the heap of bodies to search for my brothers. We pulled Tovmas' rigid body from the tangle but Gabriel was buried too deep in the grisly melee to be reached. I took Baba's watch from Tovmas' pocket, searched in vain for the key, and then Levon dragged my brother's body into the forest to scatter soil over it. I mumbled hurried prayers and lay face down on the burial mound, my pumping heart over Tovmas's silent, lacerated chest, a gold veneer of moonlight shrouding my shuddering body. I wanted to die but Levon forced me to walk with him deeper into the forest. Rose found us, some time later, slumped at the base of a tree, hanging onto life by a thread.

★★★

I am cold and shivery in spite of the sun that shines through the canopy of leaves in Ara's orchard. A vision floats before my retina: a tangle of dead boys, a living girl buried beneath them. A tear escapes. Gran's eyes come to mind, so deep and full of terrible secrets. It was in a place like this, tranquil and quiet, where birds chirruped and played among the branches, that her life was derailed. In a place just like this, her people were hunted, lay famished, dying.

A sob bubbles up through my throat, followed by a whimper, then I start to weep. When Ara draws close and wraps me in his arms, I'm overwhelmed by sadness and desire, the need to be held. I don't fight the compulsion to cry on his shoulder and nuzzle his neck, to vent my shock and grief. He kisses my cheek and I turn my face to his. He holds my gaze and moves closer. The feel of his mouth, warm and fluid, is the greatest release. I kiss Ara with a passion that burns away the unrest and banishes death from my thoughts.

Chapter 17

Katerina

I call Mum the following day to relate the next chapter of Gran's story, struggling to find the right words. Again, I'm the bearer of ill tidings and a stunned silence fills the void between us. Later, I meet Ara and we walk the seafront in a fog of thought; the bustling life on the strip emitting happy sounds at odds with the story infecting our minds.

'We need to research your Armenian name,' Ara says. 'You may have relatives you don't know about.'

'Not close ones. Gran saw her family die. We know that for sure.'

'What about her mother, the baby she was carrying?'

'You believe they survived?'

'There's always a chance. You must have distant relatives somewhere in the world. We all do.'

Ara says Gran's history is as much his as it is mine, the story of *our people*. The phrase strikes me as grandiose, at odds with the image I have of myself as a self-reliant only child, with no allegiances to any group. Ara's family history mirrors my own, his grandparents forced to flee their homes and seek refuge abroad. There's no denying this malign history is a bond, common ground. It's no surprise, he says, that Gran didn't speak about the past and only began writing her journal in later life.

'My grandfather never spoke about the past. He was a very proud man and there was no dignity in talking about beatings and starvation, the cruelty he was subjected to. '

'The past was undignified. I never thought about it like that.'

'When my grandfather came to Cyprus he had to think about making a living, learning a new language, there wasn't time to look back. I believe he wanted me to see him as a hero not a victim, perhaps your grandmother felt the same way.'

Gran was our rock, her fault lines hidden, proud of her family and the life she had carved. 'I always knew there was something dark in her makeup but I never tried to probe. Perhaps, deep down I didn't want to know.'

Ara kisses me in the street, and I respond unashamedly, setting aside habitual boundaries. I see myself from afar, pressed to his arm, and think *conveyor belt couple, holiday fling*. Only, it doesn't feel that way. Gran's story has brought us together, circumvented all the hackneyed rituals but doubts still bubble on the edge, the little voice in the back of my mind telling me to remember what happened with Rob.

At dusk, we sit on the beach, the moon bobbing on the horizon, full and orange. We listen to the waves stroke the shore, more distant sounds emanating from the strip. Mopeds whirr amidst muted strains of tavern music. It's a cool evening, still light, so different to the darkness that descends all too soon in England and chases you into bed at this time of year. Salt air mingles with the aroma of charcoaled meat, with subtle hints of honeysuckle and the scent of Ara's skin. I wish I could bottle that heady mix to take home. My outward contentment belies the sadness inside me. This attachment can be nothing but fleeting; my life in England beckoning from across the Med, The Echo, my friends, Mum.

But I need all this right now: the break, romantic respite in the sun, to listen to Gran's stories and fathom her depths. My head's filled with imagined faces of the people who shared her early life, features formed from scant descriptions, echoes of Mariam in their eyes and lips. The one I picture most vividly is Gabriel as a wide-eyed, spirited boy, quick-witted and loyal. If I could select just one person to meet from Gran's past, if such a thing were possible, it would be Great Uncle Gabriel.

Chapter 18

Gabriel, Nicosia, Cyprus.

Basturma sausages hang menacingly over my head, a dozen cumin-scented parcels, bunched like fists. I look up at them and wish they would fall and inflict a fatal blow. 'Gabriel Arakelian killed by falling basturma,' they would write on my gravestone. Gabriel Arakelian, who cheated death time and time again, was finally and thankfully seen off by a sausage. At least I will not leave this world smelling of formaldehyde but scented with eau de cumin, garlic and fenugreek. The Armenian has arrived, the dead will say, when my pungent spirit reaches the other side.

Sitting in the landlord's plastic chair, on the landlord's veranda, I knock back the last of my whisky, staring out at a small backyard furnished with a carob tree, a nest lodged in its uppermost branches. Beyond the back fence is an area of scrubland strewn with litter, home to a plethora of vermin. Marta, my wife, hurries out of the house, trailing the scent of caramelised onions, wiping wet hands on her apron.

'Go and get changed, Gabriel. Harry will be here any minute.'

'I want to die,' I tell her, assuming the hangdog look that no longer earns me sympathy.

'Wait till he's gone and you can do whatever you like,' she says, walking back into the house.

My granddaughter, Anahit, has invited her Greek boyfriend over for dinner. I wouldn't mind so much if Harry were on the menu, chopped up into tiny pieces and fricasseed. Anahit grew up in England, met the Greek while on holiday, gave up a perfectly good teaching job in Manchester to take up residence in our spare room and nurture a romance doomed to fail. She teaches history at the English School, where the upper echelons send their children, while *he* fashions wood for a living.

Marta has prepared a feast to celebrate Anahit's *announcement*, her *happy news* set to shatter a life wrought with hairline cracks. Dear God, do not let her marry a Greek. Do not let her marry a Greek. This was my mantra her whole life. Dear God, make her husband Armenian, preferably a doctor, better still a surgeon. I can only assume that my maker, the all-powerful, all-knowing creator, has a hearing impediment.

Anahit has been dating Harry for some time but we have never met, officially. I have spied on him many times from the window, picking her up in his clapped out car, headache music blaring from his quadraphonic stereo. Anyone would think I was a leper the way they keep him at a distance. My wife and Anahit consider me archaic but I am open-minded enough to accept my granddaughter has a boyfriend. Others, I know, are not so progressive.

Marta comes back, reminding me of a frenetic chicken, the way she scurries about tidying the yard, picking up stray leaves like lint from a carpet. No amount of cleaning can beautify this drab hole filled with furniture only fit for the chicken coop. The landlord is a neglectful ass and I have given up arguing with him. He is Greek too. Make of that what you will.

A cockroach scurries past my wife's feet, twitching its antennae, heading for the house. Marta spies it and with a murderous look she chases it, stamps on it twice, cracking open the exoskeleton. I am disturbed by the thought that my wife has looked at me in that exact, homicidal way and wonder if she wouldn't quite like to crush me beneath her shoe, to absent me from dinner and stop my face ruining the ambience. She pulls a tissue from her pocket and sweeps up the dead bug, firing my indignation.

'This place is a dump. Unfit for human habitation. Crawling with filthy pests.'

'Yadda, yadda, yadda. On and on you go like a scratched record.'

'My doctor says that negative feelings are better expressed than bottled up. Better out than in, congealing into tumours.'

'Everyone has roaches at this time of year, Gabriel, even the president of the Republic. They don't differentiate between rich and poor. They are egalitarian fellows just like you. The sewers are stuffed with them. Roaches are not unique to our home.'

'This is not our home, Marta. Our home lies across a barbed wire fence. It is a fine stone house with a wooden door and a spacious veranda. It is a palace compared to this place. While we live here, squatters are sitting on our sofa and pissing in our toilet and sitting at our table, stuffing their misplaced guts. I hope to God they choke.'

'I'm not going to waste my time and energy worrying about things I can't change or wishing harm on others. I certainly don't want anyone to choke on my account.'

My eye is caught by the movement of a black snake wending its way down the trunk of the carob. My old adversary, Therko, is back, sniffing for birds' eggs and our yearly battle is set to resume.

'Where is the paraffin, Marta?'

'What are you planning to do, Gabriel? Greet Harry with a burning flare?'

'No. The snake is back and this year I plan to kill it.'

'Leave the poor creature alone. It can't do any harm and it keeps down the pests you are always complaining about.'

Two years that snake has eluded me, treating this property like its private realm, slithering over rope soaked in paraffin and garlic cloves placed strategically around the yard, turning its nose up at milk laced with rat poison.

'Get up, Gabriel. Change out of those old clothes and no more talk about killing snakes. I want Harry to feel at home.'

'Pass me the yoghurt.' My request is made in Armenian, the language I have used exclusively since Harry stepped through the door. I am blessed with an ear for languages and can speak Armenian, English, Turkish and Greek.

'Grandfather, please speak Greek so Harry can

understand. How many times must I tell you?' Anahit whispers in Armenian.

'I have nothing to say,' I continue in our mother tongue to make a point, the point being that family gatherings will never be the same again with an *odar*, a foreigner, in our midst. No more cheery banter in Armenian, no more songs from the homeland, no more ribbing and teasing and arguments about politics.

A conversation full of banality and false laughter makes the hairs split on my chin. Who cares about the antics of Harry's cousin's dog which understands dozens of commands and can beg on its hind legs? Who cares about his fat, diabetic mother? I have never met his mother but Harry is full in the face and it is not unreasonable to assume, as he wolfs down Marta's lamb pilaf, that he comes from a heavy-set clan.

Marta finds Harry good looking but where she is looking, I struggle to understand, certainly not at his jowls. He is Grecian in appearance, olive-skinned, one of the common herd. Anahit is golden-haired and green-eyed, the image of my late sister, Mariam. The resemblance is uncanny and churns my heart.

A belch escapes me, a low, rumbling exhalation. The belch was unintentional but I am not displeased by its repercussions. The banalities cease. The smiles freeze, then fade. Seriousness is reasserted and the master of the house has marked his territory with a garlic-scented burst like a dog leaving the smell of piss.

Marta pulls back her chair and heads for the kitchen, smiling again. Why does she do that? Assume a look of fake happiness when there is nothing to be happy about, when today, in particular, we should both be beating our chests and howling.

'Gabriel, can you help me in the kitchen?' Marta calls out in honeyed tones.

I oblige as obediently as Harry's cousin's dog, and make my way to the kitchen where I'm met with a murderous scowl.

'Why don't you talk, Gabriel? Make the boy feel comfortable.'

'What do you want me to say?'

'I don't have a script. Use your brain. And if you belch again I will make your wish come true.'

'What wish?'

'I will wrap my hands around your wrinkled neck and squeeze the life out of you.'

Reprimand concluded, she grabs a bundle of serviettes and marches out of the kitchen. I follow, racking my brains for a question to ask a man who is far too comfortable conversing with women, yapping about dogs and his mother. He strikes me as the kind of man who would be perfectly at ease in a supermarket helping his wife choose cut-price brassieres and those sanitary unmentionables. Sitting down, I glance across at Marta, fearing her lips will split if she smiles any wider. Think, Gabriel, think, I tell myself. What question should I ask a man who clearly has no interest in politics, history, advances in medical science, whose quips are canine centred, who is as manly as a eunuch? I take the plunge.

'Is your mother fat?'

The women glare at me, Anahit's jewel eyes turning to lumps of cold onyx.

'She's not thin,' Harry says, looking amused. 'Why do you ask?'

'Because there is often a correlation between diabetes and obesity.'

'I wouldn't call her obese.'

'But she likes her food?'

'Grandfather!'

'It's OK,' Harry says. 'She's a great cook, just like your wife.' Marta looks as if she is being showered in rose water. 'She likes to cook and we like to eat.'

'That is obvious.'

'Gabriel!'

'You should watch your tendency to overeat because you may be genetically predisposed to diabetes. You don't want to suffer a stroke or go blind and be a burden to your future wife.'

'I think it's time for dessert,' Marta says, with a tight cheeriness. 'Gabriel, come and help me.'

'Don't speak, Gabriel. Don't breathe another word,' Marta hisses in the kitchen.

'Make your mind up, woman. First, you ask me to talk and when I do, you tell me to shut up.'

'You're impossible. Take the paklava and put it on the table.'

I carry out the order, feeling like a hostess trolley, hoping Harry doesn't think we are kindred, eunuch spirits. I do not cook or do women's work. I will gladly take out the rubbish and change a light bulb but ask me to shop for sanitary napkins and I will flatly refuse.

Marta follows with a bowl of rice flour pudding and, taking my seat, I turn to my wife with an innocent look.

'Is it all right to talk about snakes, my dear?'

'No,' she snaps.

'Snakes?' Harry looks interested. 'You're fond of snakes, Mr Arakelian?'

'I hate them. There's a big black one intent on stealing eggs from the nest in the carob tree.'

'It's unlikely to be poisonous and some say snakes bring good luck to a household. If you leave it alone, it won't bite.'

'Did you hear what the boy said, Gabriel? Leave that snake well alone.'

This is worse than I thought. The boy is a mealy-mouthed snake lover, and probably a deviant, pot smoker and paganist. He hunches closer to Anahit and takes her by the hand. They beam at us and my heart sinks; the hour of doom has arrived and I feel faint.

'Mr and Mrs Arakelian, Anahit and I have an announcement to make. We're getting married.'

The room swims before my eyes. Through the watery haze, I hear chairs scraping and kisses being exchanged, Marta's high-pitched exaltations. The horse has come before the cart. I was expecting them to announce their engagement, their intention to cohabit, a trial period when things can go amiss and wrong decisions can be reversed.

'Grandfather *jan*, aren't you going to congratulate us?'

'This is not how things are done in our culture.'

The room falls silent.

'This is not how things are done, Anahit. A man must ask for a woman's hand. Has he asked your father?'

'I *told* my father and he's very happy for me! It's 1985, not the turn of the century. I don't need anyone's permission but I would really like your blessing. It would mean the world to me.'

'And why the rush? Are you pregnant? I suggest you apply the brakes. You don't want to make a foolish mistake.'

'Come on, Harry, we're leaving.' She takes him by the hand and leads him to the door like a man who is soft in the head.

Marta turns to me, blinking away tears.

'I hope you're satisfied, Gabriel. Your mouth is like a runaway carriage. When will *you* learn to apply the brakes? Change your attitude or we'll lose that girl. Hasn't life taught you anything? Haven't we lost enough already?'

I go to bed with Marta's words ringing in my ears, knock back a tot of whisky to help me sleep, and sink into a restless slumber. That night I return to the clearing and see events from afar, sitting in the branches of a tree, the scene so vivid it might have happened yesterday. In the morning the visions are stuck behind my retina, float like a ghostly hologram before my eyes. A past like mine cannot be cast off like a snakeskin, it is a chronic condition, scars etched on the inside.

Chapter 19

Gabriel, Eastern Turkey, 1915

She found me three-quarters dead, the Turkish woman who was foraging for food in the forest and came across a scene straight from hell. She searched through the bodies, hoping for signs of life: a pulse, a breath, a twitch. I don't know how long I had been out cold, hours or days, before Esra freed me from the tangle of bodies and lifted me off the ground.

Images flashed through my head, snapped at my brain. My mother and Alitz appeared behind an infrared haze then faded, my father swung from a burning rope and Tovmas lay beneath a pile of bodies, a bloody hand protruding. Bright light permeated my eyelids. I felt the sun on my face and imagined I was being carried through a fertile meadow, on my way to heaven where Tovmas, Mariam and father would be waiting. I was set down, an unfamiliar softness against my back, and heard a woman's voice.

'He's burning up. I'll be surprised if he lives.'

A hint of gardenia mingled with the smell of dried blood in my nostrils. I floated in and out of consciousness. One minute I was at home in Caesaria and the next I found myself in a mud brick room, smelling of earth. I heard children's voices, saw faces, ghosts. My mother stooped to kiss my cheek and then a scarfed woman knelt beside my mattress and dabbed my face with a damp, strong smelling cloth. The wound on my cheek crusted and oozed and itched and a searing pain shot across my face. Goats and chickens gaggled in the distance, my mother singing in Armenian, young girls humming in Turkish. My lips closed around a bottle and cool water filled my mouth. I shivered from the cold and prayed for heat but when it came, it burned and left me soaked in sweat. Fragments of meaning broached my consciousness, before floating away like the feathery seeds of a dandelion swept up by the wind.

Three days later, I awoke weak but lucid. The room had bare, mud brick walls and an earth floor. A man's work clothes hung from a hook on the door. A tall dresser faced the mattress and handmade curtains framed the small window, blown by a cool breeze that carried the scent of gardenia.

A woman came into the room, the one I had seen in my dreams and who had knelt by my side. 'You're awake at last,' she spoke in Turkish. 'You must be starving. I'll fetch you something to eat.'

She laid a slice of bread in my hands, still warm. I tore into it with my teeth, suddenly aware of my ravenous hunger.

'I've spread it with fat and sprinkled on sugar,' the woman said. 'To build up your strength, my little man.'

It was the best bread I had ever tasted: sweet and salty. I collected up the crumbs on the bed, licked

81

them off my palm and yearned for more. The woman sat beside me on the mattress, watching me keenly. I flinched.

'Don't worry. I won't hurt you. Allah placed you in my path for a reason. Are you Armenian?'

I told her my name. She asked where I had come from but the past was a blur. I could remember little beyond the mattress and the bread comforting my stomach.

'Where is your family, Gabriel?'

'My family.' The past sprang back vengefully, horror filling my head, stinging my eyes, my brother and sister brought down like hunted animals. Both dead. I buried my face in my hands and sobbed. Esra took me in her arms and held me like a mother, listening to my tearful account of the slaughter in the woods, and then she wept too.

'I need to find my mother,' I said, realising suddenly that she was possibly still alive.

'It's not safe for you to leave. You will stay here until the troubles die down and then I promise to help you find your mother.'

The sound of a wagon approaching made me start and hunch close to the wall.

'Don't worry, Gabriel. That's just my husband, Ahmet, returning from the market with our daughters.'

Two young girls skipped into the room and looked surprised and nervous to see me sitting up in bed. They had wild hair, wore threadbare clothes and walked on bare feet. Their father followed them in, a big man with a thick moustache and baggy pantaloons.

'Our guest has come back to life,' Esra said. The girls applauded and the big man's face broke into a generous smile.

I spent the following week in a state of confusion, breaking down whenever I remembered my brother and sister, inert the rest of the time. I slept for much of the day or lay with my eyes closed, listening to the family go about their business. The girls playing outside, Esra grinding wheat to make flour or washing clothes in the stone sink, cooking flat bread on the brazier. I ached for my mother but having Esra close by was a comfort. I thought about returning to the clearing to bury my brother and sister but dreaded the sight of their wasted bodies. Esra had checked every child. No one else had survived.

One evening, as I lay on the mattress, floating in and out of sleep, I overheard Esra speaking to her husband in the next room.

'I want to keep him, Ahmet. To raise him as my own. The poor boy has no one.'

'I'd like that too but I'm afraid. Today, I heard the village mayor was removed from his post for giving refuge to Armenian children. What happens if they find Gabriel?'

'I don't care. I love him.'

'What if they find him? Think of the girls.'

'Noone will find him out here. If anyone asks, I will tell them the boy is my sister's son. He speaks Turkish as well as we do.'

'We're playing with fire.'

83

'I won't give him up, Ahmet. I won't send him to his death. I couldn't live with myself.'

The next morning Esra walked to the village with her daughters on an errand. I stared from the window, my mind shutting down as it often did. I preferred not to think, not to dwell on the recent past. The sound of a horse-drawn cart woke me from my stupor and, moments later, Ahmet pulled up outside the house. He was a farm labourer and usually worked into the evening. His return was unexpected.

He beckoned me over. 'Let me take you for a ride, Gabriel.'

Esra had warned me to stay indoors, not to answer the door if she was out, not to tell anyone I was Armenian. But I trusted Ahmet and was glad of the chance to escape the house where I lived like a fugitive.

The dirt road leading away was narrow and furrowed. The wheels of the rickety cart clattered over bumps, unsettling my stomach. I sensed Ahmet's nervousness as he drove the old horse along the rough path that skirted the forest and then wove through it. I sensed this was not a casual drive, that Ahmet was heading somewhere with a sense of purpose. Thirty minutes later, I saw the point of a minaret rising over the treetops before a small mosque came into view.

'Where are we going, Ahmet?' Panic set my limbs quivering.

'Somewhere safe. Don't worry.'

A turbaned mullah, with a broad, disarming smile, strode towards the wagon and Ahmet pulled on the reins and turned to me. 'The mullah has promised to take you to a safe house in Beirut. Somewhere you will find other Armenian orphans.'

'I don't want to go.' I wasn't ready to leave the safety of Esra's home and the family I trusted.

'Climb down, boy,' the mullah said. 'Noone here wants to hurt you.'

'But I haven't said goodbye to Esra.'

'She doesn't know I've taken you,' Ahmet said. 'Please forgive me, Gabriel. I had to put the safety of my family first.'

'Climb down, boy. We have a long journey ahead of us and must set off before nightfall.' The mullah took my hand in his bony fingers.

'Please look after this boy,' Ahmet said. 'My wife and I have grown to love him.'

The mullah waved him away before leading me into the mosque.

Chapter 20

Gabriel, Nicosia

'...*Your mouth is like a runaway carriage*, Marta said.' My friend, Partogh, listens with a wry smile, shaking dice in his cupped hand. 'She has been giving me the cold shoulder for days.'

We are at the Armenian club, an oasis of leather chairs moulded by bony and fleshy derrieres, a harbour for retired males addicted to the roll and clatter of dice. Smoke floats like cumulonimbus overhead. The invigorating smell of coffee and sugar-dusted tahini rolls wafts from the kitchenette.

Partogh throws a double six, moving his counters with an unsettling smirk.

'Why are you smiling, Partogh? What's so funny? My wife isn't speaking to me. My granddaughter is intent on marrying an *odar*. Your friend is in the doghouse, being thrown the occasional bone for dinner. Marta hasn't cooked lamb in five days, only beans and cracked wheat. I am on the brink of starvation, man, suffering chronic flatulence. If it weren't for the cream turnovers at the club, I would pass out. Why in God's name are you looking so happy?'

'I threw two sixes.'

'You smiled before you threw the double.'

'I had a premonition.'

'Are you gratified by your friend's misfortune?'

'The misfortune you create.'

'What do you mean?'

'You are an old dog, Gabriel. Your own worst enemy.'

'I am starting to hate even the mention of dogs since the Greek is so fond of them.'

Another double wins Partogh the game and I sit back in my seat, light a Rothmans and take a long, satisfying drag. The club is bustling, alive with the sound of political debate. Raised voices reverberate. Our friend, Hovsepian, comes across and sits in the vacant chair, sucking on his pipe. I tell him my woes and, just as I expect, he is more sympathetic.

'You did the right thing, Gabriel. I would have done far worse. If my granddaughter brings home a Greek, I will disinherit her.'

'Then you're an ass, Hovsepian,' Partogh says. 'The Greeks are our brothers.'

Hovsepian blows air through his nose. 'They don't understand our traditions or feel our music or speak our language or eat our food.'

'They eat souvla, we eat khorovatz, in other words, meat threaded onto skewers cooked over a barbecue. They eat koubebia, we eat sarmas. Both dishes comprise stuffing wrapped inside a vine leaf. What's the difference? A few pignoli nuts? That's hardly cause for apartheid.'

'You're the one who's nuts, Partogh. Nuts. Nuts. Nuts.' Hovsepian emphasises his point with an expressive twist of his fingers against his temple. 'If all our young people follow in Anahit's footsteps, there will be no Armenian speakers left in twenty years and we, as a race, will cease to exist.'

Partogh sighs. 'Sacrifice for the greater good, as you say, time and time again. You make me sick. What about that unpredictable variable called love, Hovsepian? Where does that come into your scheme of things?'

'After family duty, of course.'

'How would you like it if your granddaughter married an *odar*?' I ask.

'It's not what I would wish for but her happiness comes before mine. Gabriel, at least your daughter married an Armenian.'

Hovsepian exhales a plume of pungent smoke. 'Well, you can think what you like. If my granddaughter marries an *odar*, she will get nothing. Not a penny.'

'I have nothing to give so I can hardly make threats like that,' I say.

Hovsepian nods sympathetically and then an idea appears to strike him. 'That might just be your saving grace, my friend. When the Greek realises there is no money in the Arakelian account, no land to build on, he may reassess the situation. You know how money-minded these Greeks are.'

'Our community is going exactly the same way,' Partogh says. 'We are rapidly becoming an incorrigible gaggle of nouveau riche.'

'Speak for yourself,' Hovsepian says.

'The only thing of value I own is my watch and he's not getting his hands on it.' A silver pocket watch hangs from the buttonhole of my waistcoat, bought for one thousand Cyprus pounds from a dealer, back in the days when I had spare cash, a copy of the timepiece my father once owned.

'Just think, Gabriel. When Anahit gets married, you may finally get that great grandson you've always been harping on about, the one who will take your name and go to medical school.'

Hovsepian scoffs. 'And never speak a word of our language.'

A woman walks into the club and all eyes turn to stare, not in a lascivious way but more suspicious, resentful of the intrusion. She approaches the club president who shakes her hand.

'Who's that?' I ask. 'I don't recognise her. Looks a bit of a mess, probably English.'

The president turns and points a finger at me.

'Why the hell are they looking at me? I come here to get away from women. What does the president think he's doing?'

'We'll find out soon enough, Gabriel. They're coming over,' Partogh says.

'Gentlemen,' the president adopts the Queen's English. 'I would like to introduce you to Jennifer from California.'

'I told you she was an *odar*,' I say, in Armenian.

'Jennifer is an anthropologist,' the president says. 'She is conducting a detailed study on the Armenian diaspora and would like to concentrate on our community here in Cyprus. She would like to speak to as many of us as possible – about our lives now and in the past, our social networks, that kind of thing.'

'I'm not a guinea pig to be poked and prodded by a woman whose ridiculous hair makes her look like an artichoke gone to seed.'

Hovsepian chuckles at my quip in Armenian.

'I am truly delighted to meet you all,' Jennifer says with typically fake American exuberance. On what premise does she base her delight at meeting me?

'Gabriel.' The president singles me out again. 'You have a very interesting tale to tell. Perhaps you would be prepared to give Jennifer a little of your time?'

'I'm playing backgammon.'

'I wouldn't dream of disturbing you, right now, Mr . . . ' Jennifer says.

'Arakelian.'

'Perhaps I could make an appointment for later on today or tomorrow. Whenever's most convenient. There's no desperate rush. I'm here for several weeks.'

'Why don't you go to Gabriel's house this afternoon,' Partogh says. 'His wife is a lovely woman and I'm sure she would be more than happy to help you. Is five o'clock convenient for you, my friend?'

I don't know why but I nod, albeit resentfully. At five I drink coffee, read the paper and sit with my feet up, dressed in my vest and slippers.

'That would be wonderful. Thank you. And how would you like me to do my hair next time we meet, Mr Arakelian? I would hate to look like a vegetable.'

'I'm sorry?'

'Gabriel. I forgot to mention that Jennifer is a fluent

Armenian speaker. Isn't she clever?' The president grins, ape like, his words dangling in the air like a pack of monkeys in a tree.

Partogh splutters a laugh and Hovsepian chokes on a mouthful of smoke.

Chapter 21

Gabriel, Beirut, 1916

I dreamt I was at home in Caesaria, lying on my back in bed beside Mariam. She whispered a joke and I smothered my laughter by covering my face with the bed sheet. I feared the dark and my sister's warm presence made me feel safe. With Mariam's banter playing over in my mind, I woke up with a smile on my face. It faded the second I opened my eyes and found myself transposed; lifting my head and glancing around I despaired, realising, as if for the first time, that I would only ever see Mariam in dreams, that my father was gone and my mother was as good as dead. I tried to sleep, to spirit myself back to Caesaria but the sound of weeping, snoring, coughing, of boys passing wind, firmly anchored me to the reality of my new life where I had an assumed identity, where my name had been changed to Guven.

After Ahmet had dropped me off at the mosque, I had travelled with the mullah to the orphanage in Beirut where I had been living for just over a year. I still missed Esra, though I had known her for so little time, and often thought about the angel woman who had saved my life and shown me great kindness.

The bell rang for Morning Prayer in the refectory. Four hundred orphaned boys shifted wearily from their oblong strips of bedding. Sweat, must and urine pervaded the stuffy air. All our heads were shaved to rid us of lice but the parasites festered in other places: bedding, clothes and the sparse underarm hair of the older boys.

Bright sunlight streamed through the arched, stone windows of this former college and seminary. Dust mites, as small as the diseased parasites that gorged on young blood, twirled in the flood of light. Most of the boys in the orphanage were Armenian but there were orphaned Turkish and Kurdish children too, living beneath the beamed ceiling of the three-hundred-year-old building with its vast, vaulted rooms, long corridors and shaded cloisters. The year before, Lazarist priests had walked the halls with heads lowered, reading the scriptures. Expelled by the Ottoman governor, the priests had moved to a monastery at a higher altitude on Mount Lebanon.

I dressed hurriedly, pulling on a white robe and sleeveless grey coat. There were shouts from the far end of the room. I viewed the ensuing commotion with dispassion. Yeprem, an Armenian boy, was lying curled up on his side, refusing to get up, his bedding stained with vomit. His older brother, Minas, was bent over, urging him to Morning Prayer, before the guards came and dragged him out of bed. The orphanage was run with military precision and harsh punishments were inflicted on those who defied its rules. It was staffed by Turkish soldiers, guards, officers, inspectors and teachers. Four Arab nuns were charged with overseeing the hygiene and nutrition of 800 boys.

Yeprem complained of stomach ache and began to cry. Boys crowded round the mattress, chanting, *get up, get up*. The brothers were popular, Minas in particular. He could beat any boy at arm wrestling, argue his case like the best politician. He had sandy hair and clever eyes, the colour of molasses. There were rumours that he was planning to escape. A Kurdish boy approached, his arms folded across his chest. His name was Munzir and he was the leader of a small group of Kurdish orphans.

'Tell your brother to shut up. I'm sick of his wailing.' Munzir glanced at the small boys who trailed him, children who admired his nerve and saw him as a father figure.

Minas tried to pull his brother out of bed.

'He's not going anywhere but an early grave,' Munzir said. 'Why don't you let him die and give us all a rest from his terrible squawking?'

Minas' eyes burned. He pulled a fork from his pocket and plunged it into Munzir's arm. The Kurdish orphan cried out, yanked the fork from his flesh and threw himself onto Minas, knocking him over. The boys rolled across bedding, punching, scratching, and biting. Spit and blood flew through the air, streaking the floor and the robes of the boys who chanted their support, giving vent to their stifled passions. Within minutes, Minas had Munzir pinned down and was slamming his head on the ground. I feared the shouts and screams would alert the guards, that ultimately

Minas would lose this fight even if he walked away the victor.

Munzir's head thrashed from side to side as he tried to free himself and loosen the hands that gripped his throat. He gasped, his face turning red, his bulging eyes begging Minas to release him. I heard the rapid stomp of Alim's boots before I saw the guard throw open the door of the dormitory and storm in. Minas was quickly rustled to his feet and hidden behind a group of Armenian boys.

'What happened here?' The guard stood over Munzir who writhed on the ground, clutching his neck.

No one spoke. Alim grabbed a small boy by the arm. 'Tell me what happened or you will all be punished.'

He shook the boy like a rag doll until urine pooled at his feet and he begged the guard to stop. Minas stepped forward, his face wet and bloody. 'We had a fight,' he said.

'What's your name?'

'Minas Eghian.'

I held my breath, thinking Minas at once foolish and heroic for defying orphanage rules by referring to his Armenian name. Every Armenian boy was assigned a Turkish name on entering the orphanage. Some of the younger boys had forgotten their family names, their language, and their religion. They had been successfully deconstructed and remoulded. They prayed to Allah five times a day, considered the mullah their spiritual leader and marched with gusto up and down the stone courtyard, to please the orphanage director who looked on with satisfaction, proud of his role in converting the *gyavours*, the non-believers.

'What did you say?' The guard gripped the handle of the wooden club tucked beneath the sash round his waist.

'I said my name is Minas Eghian.'

Alim drew the club and swiped Minas across the head, wood thudding against bone. Minas was knocked off his feet for the second time that morning and lay stunned, his face to the ground.

'Now, have you remembered your name?'

My stomach clenched. I willed Minas to back down and save himself, to stop defying the guard who wielded ultimate power and seemed to gain pleasure unleashing his anger with a club or leather strap.

Minas stood up and straightened his back, his jaw tight, his eyes reflecting the guard's hostile glare. 'My name is Minas Eghian.'

Alim grabbed him roughly by the arm and dragged him out of the room while the older boys clenched their fists and held back tears.

After Morning Prayer in the refectory, and a breakfast of bread and olives, I took up my duties as assistant to Doctor Bahar in the orphanage hospital where several dozen boys were being treated. Looking after the sick, I managed to forget my past life for long stretches of the day and live only in the present. I had a good command of Turkish and no longer lapsed into Armenian, though I thought and dreamed in Armenian.

My first job of the day was to administer calcium

sulphide grains to the boys showing signs of typhus, those with high temperatures and abdominal pain, with hacking coughs and a dull rash on their bodies. The room was overcrowded and ill equipped. Sick boys lay on stained mattresses. They coughed up blood and mucus into dirty rags. Some lay motionless, burned by fever, their bodies sapped of fluid. Others suffered agonising pain. I had grown accustomed to the fetid stench of sickness and the hiss of laboured breath that signalled death.

Entering the sickroom, I wasn't surprised to see Yeprem lying on a mattress near the door, staring up at the ceiling, his face drained of colour, a soiled robe clinging to his emaciated body.

Doctor Bahar was deep in thought, stroking his grey beard. He stood over Yeprem. 'Guven, my boy, the situation is serious. This typhus outbreak is getting out of hand. Another day, another casualty and I expect there will be more before nightfall.'

'Yes, *effendi*.' The doctor had always been kind, treating me with respect, rewarding my help with gifts of food. He knew my father had been a doctor but was surprised by my medical knowledge.

'Why do the orphans come to me only when their symptoms are so advanced? Why don't they come earlier when they can be treated and saved?'

I knew the answer to the doctor's question but I shrugged in reply. The orphans believed Doctor Bahar was poisoning his patients on the orders of the director. The doctor was a good man, did all he could to treat the sick with our few medical supplies. He improvised with the contents of apothecary jars left behind by the Lazarist priests, using ointments, pills and tinctures sparingly. The best he could do for most was administer morphine to alleviate pain, numb their senses and ease them into death.

Two guards arrived, looking warily around the room, fearing contagion. The doctor pointed to a boy lying on a mattress in the corner of the hospital. The guards muttered curses under their breath, aggrieved they had been sent to bury another infectious orphan. They made their way across the room, wrapped the dead boy in his sheet and carried him away. This scene played out several times a week in the orphanage hospital and I had come to regard death as commonplace. I had stopped mourning the orphans headed for shallow graves or the nearest river, to be dispatched from the world without religious ceremony.

At midday the sickroom felt stuffy, airless and hot, in spite of the open windows. A number of boys had rolled from their bedding onto the floor in an effort to cool themselves, pressing their cheeks against stone. Sweat beaded on my forehead and trickled down my body while the soporific heat seeped into my bones.

The hospital door opened and Alim dragged Minas into the room by the leg. He was naked to the waist, his body scalded raw. I had seen other boys in this condition, a consequence of being forced to stand and stare at the sun for hours. Minas' skin would blister and his eyes might be damaged beyond repair. The sun was crueller than the guards, burning the eye in the same way that a magnifying glass, held up to bright sunlight, scorched paper.

Alim dropped his captive's leg. It flopped to the ground and buckled. 'Where shall I put this boy?'

'Just leave him to us. You've done your job,' the doctor replied, sternly, unafraid to show his disapproval. When Alim left the room, Doctor Bahar took a closer look at Minas and shook his head. 'Isn't there enough sickness in this place without those idiots creating more? Where shall we put this poor boy?'

A week passed. Minas and Yeprem were recovering well. Yeprem slept while his brother sat opposite me on the floor. We played a game with small stones. Minas' stones were a Russian battalion. He lined them up and waited for me to assemble the Turkish army, before the stones hurled themselves at one another and scattered. Beyond the walls of the orphanage real soldiers fought with weapons that tore through flesh. Inside the compound there was little mention of war. We hungered for information and tuned into our teachers' whispered conversations. Occasionally, the doctor volunteered information, expressing his dismay that the Turkish army had suffered terrible losses and were on the retreat.

In spite of myself, I had let down my guard and come to think of Minas as a friend. I admired his courage but feared his recklessness.

'Friend,' he whispered. 'Please do what you can to help Yeprem. We're leaving on Sunday.'

'Where are you going?'

'We're paying a guard to help us escape. Why don't you come with us?'

The idea of escaping struck me as impossible. 'Where did you get the money?'

'I make belts from scraps of leather and sell them.' Minas was being trained in shoemaking and managed to scavenge scraps to make the belts he sold on the black market. The orphans exchanged whatever currency they could get their hands on: food, steel wire, cloth, knives and forks for protection. Some sold bread to the starving Lebanese civilians who begged for food at the compound gate.

It was late afternoon and the humid breeze on my skin felt like warm breath. I stood in the courtyard waiting for Minas who had gone in search of materials. A clock tower loomed behind me, a giant, stone edifice topped by a turreted wall, so tall it could be seen from miles around. A statue of St Joseph, holding a carpenter's square, was set in a deep alcove beneath a clock that no longer chimed.

Minas returned with several stones, a length of wire, a fragment of broken glass and a piece of cloth, filched from a basket outside the nuns' sewing room. He led me to the back of the building and onto a window ledge. Jutting bricks, stone ledges, a small alcove and a balcony were the footholds we used to climb the side of the building before pulling ourselves onto the roof. I fought my fear and struggled to lift the weight of my own body until, eventually, I was shuffling along the roof's summit with Minas sauntering ahead.

'How can you walk so quickly? Aren't you afraid of falling?' I lagged behind, losing my footing several times.

'I've been up here hundreds of times. I love being up high.'

Minas reached a flat section of roof, above a row of vacant storerooms. I slumped down beside him and saw what I had so far failed to notice because I had been too busy watching my feet. A fertile mountain of evergreens spread over the horizon, a mountain I had barely looked at since arriving at the orphanage because I had no interest in the outside world. From this elevated platform lay a biblical landscape, with forests of juniper, carob and pine, a mountainside pulsating with birdlife, where generations had lived in stone houses and foraged for almonds, pistachios and honey. Perched on top of the building, I felt strong and invincible, no longer at the mercy of the headmaster, the teachers or Alim. Looking out at the world from this vantage point, hope flooded my heart and I desperately wanted to be free.

'I'm leaving with you on Sunday,' I said. 'Tell me what I have to do, what I need to bring.'

'Nothing. I have everything ready and hidden in a safe place. Somewhere the guards won't search. It's not going to be easy. We'll have to move fast and cover our tracks and it's not just the guards we have to fear.'

'What do you mean?'

'There are wolves, jackals and wildcats out there.' Minas motioned towards the mountain. 'And they are all as hungry as we are.'

Minas took a piece of folded leather from inside his shoe and placed it on the ground, then set to unravelling the cloth to make thread that he wound into a ball. Next, he filed the end of the wire with a stone to form a sharp point before flattening the other side, folding it over and rubbing it with the glass to create a tiny hole. Watching my friend at work, making a needle, threading it and beginning to sew, I felt a growing sense of peace, tinged with guilt. When I had left my brother and sister in the clearing, I had never expected to feel contentment again, but in the company of Minas, tucked away from the regimented world below, with the early evening breeze cooling my face, I felt alive, imbued with the spirit of the boy from Caesaria. I breathed in the pine-scented air and began to plan my future because, in that moment, everything seemed possible. I would escape with Minas on Sunday, I would find my mother and we would all travel to America and embark on a new life.

Three nights before the planned escape, I couldn't sleep. I was so deep in thought that I didn't hear the gentle pad of bare feet making their way towards me through the maze of bedding. I felt a tap on my arm and turned to see Minas crouching beside his mattress.

'Get up. I have something to show you,' he whispered.

Pulling on my robe, I followed him out of the dormitory, tripping over an outstretched leg, cursing my clumsiness. Munzir was awake and leaning on his elbows, he watched two dark shapes making their way across the room. As soon as we had gone, he got up and felt his way along the dormitory walls. He hurried down the wide stone staircase and headed for Alim's hut to report the infringement, to win favour with the guard and sort out Minas, once and for all.

A cold breeze prickled my skin as Minas and I crept through the colonnaded walkway that spanned the length of the building. The darkness had thinned and we kept to the shadows. Minas led me through a hazelnut grove towards a small, abandoned chapel with a domed roof. Brushing aside the thorny branches of a hawthorn tree, Minas pushed open the arched door and squeezed through. I followed and was struck by a sight I had not anticipated. Three enormous stained glass windows, dimly lit by the early morning sun, bathed the stone walls, the altar table and the pulpit in shades of red, mauve and amber. The allegorical design on the mosaic and the faint smell of incense and candle wax transported me to the church of St Gregory, where I had worshipped every Sunday with my parents, where I had worn the robes of an altar boy and sang in the choir beside Tovmas.

'Come on,' Minas said. 'We don't have much time. The morning bell will ring soon.'

Minas led me to a small, windowless side room at the foot of the church where the smell of incense was more pronounced. While I stood blinking into darkness, Minas lit a candle and held it up, casting light on a room strung with cobwebs and littered with objects left by the departing priests: pieces of burgundy velvet, several broken candles and an incense burner. Minas drew the candle close to a wooden dresser and pulled at a piece of wood that looked like a fixed divider between the drawers, revealing a secret compartment filled with coins.

'This is where I keep my money. Noone else knows. I haven't even told my brother.'

'Why not?'

'He's not good at keeping secrets.'

'I won't tell anybody.'

'If anything happens to me, Gabriel, promise me you'll take my brother and leave, just as we've arranged.'

'Nothing will happen to you.'

'I won't let them beat me again. I would rather die than be made to stand and stare at the sun again.'

The chapel door creaked open. Alim entered. Minas quickly snuffed out the candle, replaced the drawer and told me to run. We tore past the guard and made our escape. Alim chased us through the hazelnut grove, along the dirt track behind the nun's dormitory and across the stone floor of the arched walkway. I stopped to catch my breath and he ran past me, intent on netting the boy who refused to live by the rules, who had failed to learn his lesson, who climbed the orphanage building like a lizard. Alim clambered after him, shouting, waking the boys, the teachers, the nuns. Children gathered at the first floor windows and craned their necks to watch Minas scaling the clock tower.

I called out in Armenian, saying words I hadn't spoken aloud for many months, begging Minas to come down but my friend was deaf to the world and intent on escaping Alim. He climbed the wooden slats of the fourth storey window and reached for the turret wall, hauling himself over the rim and stepping onto the flat roof. The boys at the dormitory window screamed their support, drowning out my voice, spurring Minas on.

Alim had climbed as high as he dared and stood on the roof waiting for Minas to surrender. Hearing the commotion, Doctor Bahar had run out of the building in his nightshirt and joined the small crowd gathered in the courtyard.

'Take a good look around,' Alim shouted, a hand on his club. 'When I've finished with you, your eyes won't be of any use.'

Minas stepped onto the rim of the turret wall where he balanced shakily, his arms outstretched. A gasp rose from the crowd while the youngest modified their calls, begging Minas to climb down. Munzir stood amidst boys who jostled for space at the window, fear slivering his eyes. He had not meant for this to happen. Yeprem was still lying in his bed, stirring into consciousness, unaware that his brother stood on a precipice 200 feet high.

'There's only one way down,' Alim shouted, but Minas knew there was another route.

As I looked on, my heart pounding in my ears, Minas stepped forward and dropped like overripe fruit, the dull thud silencing onlookers momentarily before the nuns started to scream and the eyes at the window flowed with tears.

Minas lay twisted, his limbs jutting at queer angles as if he were a wooden puppet with pins at each joint. Blood trickled from his mouth and a clear liquid seeped from a crack in his skull. My hardened stomach churned and I was violently sick. In the moments that followed, I remembered my father on the gallows, my siblings in the clearing and all my pain gathered into one monstrous mass that made me sink to my knees, bury my head in my hands and sob. Doctor Bahar gently pulled me to my feet and led me back to the orphanage to save me the sight of my friend's broken body being tugged away and slung into the back of a horse-drawn cart.

Three days later, in bed, my mind spooled back to the scene on the clock tower. This recurrent image kept me awake, tossing and turning on the mattress. I tried to think clearly, to remember the details of the escape plan, but my thoughts ran along a series of jumbled tracks that led back to the same frame. I was dressed and ready to go but had to wait until the dormitory was silent and still. Then, I would collect Yeprem from the hospital and the money from the chapel and meet the guard who was aiding our escape at the crumbling section of wall behind the kitchen block. I would need all the strength I could muster to convince Yeprem to stand and walk. He was devastated by the death of his brother and had lost the will to live.

Grief had blinded me to the goings-on in the orphanage. Something significant had passed me by. I carried out my duties in the hospital mechanically, barely registering the doctor's constantly lined and furrowed face. I paid little attention to the director's absence from the refectory at lunchtime, the easing of rules in the classroom, the sudden disappearance of several members of high ranking staff, including the head teacher. I turned my back on the boys who shared their suspicions, thinking only of my lost friend and escape.

That night, the Armenians played Chinese Whispers again, theorising and speculating, while a body plummeted before my open eyes. It was vital I stayed awake and honoured my promise to Minas, but as the dormitory fell silent, tiredness overwhelmed me.

The next morning, I was woken by the heat of the sun warming my face. I shot to my feet in a panic. I had slept through the night and missed my opportunity to escape. Looking around, I grew confused and disorientated. The dormitory was empty but I hadn't heard the bell ring and no one had woken me for Morning Prayer. I dressed hurriedly and headed for the refectory where the other boys were already standing at their tables. There were no teachers on the raised platform, no director, no mullah and no guards. I took my place and waited until Doctor Bahar walked into the room and asked us to sit. All eyes rested on the doctor's face as he stopped suddenly and put his hand on the shoulder of an older boy.

'My son, Ahmet, what was your Armenian name?' His weary eyes fixed on the puzzled boy's.

'It was Adroushan, *effendi*.'

The doctor scanned the room, settling his gaze on me. 'And you Guven, my son, what is your Armenian name?'

'My name is Gabriel, *effendi*. Gabriel Arakelian.'

'Starting from today, this morning, right now, you are all Armenians again and you have no masters here. We are no longer the rulers of this region.'

The boys cheered and the doctor raised his hand, asking for silence, glancing at the tables where the

Kurdish and Turkish orphans sat anxiously, where Munzir looked terrified.

'The only thing I ask is that you all continue to live in peace with one another as you have done for so many years.'

Adroushan turned to the doctor. 'Since, we have no masters here, we can do as we please.'

This pronouncement unleashed the boys from their bonds. Incredulous, they laughed and cheered, and quickly dispersed. I felt immune to joy and thought only of my friend and how close he had come to winning his freedom.

The doctor approached. 'I'm pleased for you, Gabriel. I hope we can remain friends.'

'Why did you stay, *effendi*? Why didn't you leave with the others?'

'There are still sick boys here and I have a duty to look after them.'

'Why don't you go home to your family?'

'I have no family, Gabriel. My wife and two sons are dead. They were killed by the Russians. You would all be dead too if I had followed the orders of the director. He told me to poison the food last night, but I couldn't do it. All I have ever wanted to do is save life, just like your father.'

The orphans spent the day ransacking the classrooms, the teachers' living accommodation, and the director's office. They smashed windows, ate all the food, quickly established their own pecking order and built fires, burning their textbooks, their desks and the clubs and leather straps used to punish them. The reprisals began almost immediately with Munzir becoming the first victim of the vigilantes. Word had spread about his role in Minas' death and he was taken to the woods by a group of boys, led by the grieving brother, and beaten senseless.

Late in the evening the Red Cross arrived with a Catholic priest and an Arab sheriff. Doctor Bahar was handcuffed and led away. I headed for the domed chapel in the walnut grove and prayed for Minas, wondering what would happen to the doctor.

Several months later, at a military court hearing, a dozen orphans testified that children had been poisoned in the orphanage hospital with lethal injections administered by Doctor Bahar. I testified too, in his defence, but my voice was drowned out by the majority and the kindly doctor, who had saved so many lives, was sentenced to death by firing squad.

Chapter 22

Gabriel, Nicosia

Jennifer, the anthropologist, comes at the agreed time with her notebook and Dictaphone, finding me preened and wearing a suit at Marta's insistence. I followed the barked command, in the hope of being forgiven for the crime of letting my mouth run away with me.

Jennifer's hair is now more pineapple than artichoke, still gathered but a little less messy. 'Thank you so much for allowing me into your home.' Her Armenian is perfect but for the drawling twang and, I have to admit, I am more than a little impressed.

'How did you learn to speak Armenian so well, my dear?' Marta asks.

'My husband taught me. Joseph Kerdian. You may have heard of him. He's a maths professor and a keen traveller. He gave a talk at your community centre several years ago about his trip to Mount Ararat.'

'You are the wife of Kerdian?'

'The one and only. He gave me the idea of studying your community. He has many relatives in Cyprus. He loves the place.'

I find myself warming to Jennifer, overlooking her hair.

'Is my hair to your liking this afternoon, Mr Arakelian?' She reads my mind.

'That's an odd question, my dear,' Marta says.

'Earlier today Mr Arakelian described me as looking like an artichoke gone to seed. A wonderful metaphor. My husband found it hilarious. He can't wait to meet you.'

'You told your husband?'

'Gabriel! Jennifer has lovely hair.'

'Actually, I have alopecia. I tie my hair up to hide the bald patch.'

My wife's scowl tells me I am back in dog land and will stay there for some time.

Marta fetches a tray laden with tea and halva rolls and chats to Jennifer as if they are long lost friends reunited. Within minutes, Jennifer discovers we have a daughter called Tamar, mother of three, who lives in England with her architect husband. That our grand-daughter Anahit *fell in love* while on holiday in Cyprus and will soon be marrying a talented Greek carpenter who makes one-offs, works of practical art, she calls them, adorning the foyer of the municipal library and the mansions of the rich and famous. A carpenter! How closely I will have to guard this terrible secret from my friends, especially Hovsepian, whose granddaughter is married to a dentist.

'Do you have children?' Marta asks.

Jennifer shakes her head.

'How old are you?' I ask.

'Thirty-nine.'

'Put your career aside, young lady. You don't have many child bearing years left.'

'I can't have children, Mr Arakelian.'

111

'Why not? Do you have ovulation problems?'

'Gabriel, you're being intrusive.'

'It's OK, Mrs Arakelian. I've been asked every question under the sun by doctors trying to find the root of the problem. My husband and I have had countless tests and examinations but there doesn't seem to be a physical reason for our inability to conceive.'

'Have you tried eating pomegranate?' Marta says.

I splutter a laugh. 'Why don't you tell her to stand on her head after sex?'

'Do you have to be so coarse, Gabriel?'

'Do you have to be so medieval, woman?'

'Perhaps you should try Evening Primrose Oil.'

'Believe me, Mrs Arakelian, I've tried everything, even standing on my head. I would love to have a child but I've had to accept that I never will.'

'Don't give up, my dear. There's no better feeling in the world than having a child.'

Unless the child of that child is hell-bent on breaking your heart.

'What exquisite figurines,' Jennifer says, eyeing Marta's small collection of glass animals.

'I had quite a few more before we lost our home.'

'Marta spent twenty years building up a collection. She had a whole menagerie, a veritable zoo.'

'I'm sorry to hear that.'

'It's such a small thing to lose in the general scheme of things,' Marta says. 'I have my husband and my family – that's all that really matters to me.'

'Shall we make a start?' Jennifer asks. 'And do you mind if I record the interview?'

'Not at all,' Marta says and Jennifer presses a button on her Dictaphone, her eye caught by the framed picture on the wall, the cherished half photograph of my father. 'Who's that elegant man?' she asks.

'My father. It was taken on his wedding day.'

'And your mother?'

'Lost with all the rest of my childhood possessions. I'd give anything for just a glimpse of my mother's face but that will never happen.' I remember the day I tore that photo down the middle, giving half to Mariam because I couldn't bear to part with my father.

Pictures adorn the walls of our home, eternal images of Tamar and Aharon, my three grandchildren, every milestone captured: birthdays, Christmases, christenings, weddings, graduations, holidays on the island, my granddaughters in swimsuits and evening dresses, performing in school plays, playing instruments, sitting in the backyard eating wedges of watermelon. Professional pictures taken during my time as a photographer, badly framed shots snapped by their parents, duplicates on celluloid stored in a filing cabinet. I won't be caught out again.

'Mr Arakelian, you may begin now, wherever you wish.'

Chapter 23

Gabriel, Mediterranean Sea, 1919

Six months after the orphanage was liberated, I found myself aboard a sailboat crowded with refugees headed for Cyprus. Armenian families packed the deck, sitting on rugs and cushions, huddled around their few possessions. The First World War had ended and displaced people around the world were rebuilding their lives. Armenians sought out safe havens, joining relations in Europe and America, our plight a footnote in history, dwarfed by the calamity of world war.

I had been sick several times over the side of the wooden vessel and sat curled up in a corner. The sea was calm but my stomach grumbled and convulsed, upset by the rocking motion and my feelings of insecurity. I had grown accustomed to the orphanage rules and regulations, to the faces I had woken up to every morning. I was a released prisoner, overwhelmed and unsettled by my strange, newfound freedom. The previous day, I had watched the shoreline of my homeland disappear from view, thinking of my mother. I was convinced she was still alive and wondered how she would find me across a stretch of interminable sea that left no track to follow.

Life at the orphanage had been transformed following

the arrival of the Red Cross and then the Lazarist priests, who set about restoring the boys' Armenian identities. The Turkish and Kurdish boys were sent to an orphanage in Syria while the rest of us were tutored by priests and volunteer Armenian teachers. A team of American missionaries arrived to run the school and tend the sick. Medicines were administered by efficient nurses in starched white uniforms. A woman called Miss Templeton became head of the school, a maternal figure who encouraged us to draw, to paint, to document our experiences on paper and spur the process of catharsis. I had hardly spoken since my friend's death and remained withdrawn in spite of Miss Templeton's efforts.

Slowly, the adults earned our trust and the sharp objects kept in pockets for protection were gradually surrendered. Miss Templeton sent the most gifted boys to a college in the region to begin their formal education. Yeprem was sent with the money his brother had saved and I was offered a scholarship.

The day before I was due to leave, Miss Templeton invited me into her office. My mother's brother, Nareg, had been found, working as an asbestos miner in Cyprus. Miss Templeton had forwarded a list of the boys' names to Armenian parishes around the world and my uncle had come across my name. The good news was tinged with disappointment. The person I wanted most of all was still missing.

I hugged my knees as I stared at a young boy sleeping in his mother's arms, the security he felt visible in the smoothness of his face. Many of the boys at the orphanage had acquired adult faces, tough and savage. I wondered if my features had also been hardened by the years spent without a family's love. The boy stirred and his mother rocked him gently, lulling him back to sleep, stroking his head with a tenderness that choked my throat. I had never felt so envious, so resentful.

I looked out into the airy distance, trying to summon good memories but only stabbing thoughts would come: Mariam's body turned to bone, scattered fragments of meta-carpals and phalanges buried like fallen twigs beneath a pelt of earth. I tried to conjure a living version of my sister, a beautiful ghost with glowing olive skin. The sea was a blue canvas in flux. I stared hard at the evolving shapes and by sheer force of will, Mariam rose like salt spray in a dress of white foam, her dark hair fanning out as she leapt up and twirled, before melting into the ocean. She came at my bidding and left of her own volition, as fleetingly as many other ghosts that lurked on the periphery of my consciousness.

I focused my gaze on the horizon, saline air stinging my eyes, until several hours later the minarets on Larnaca's shoreline came into view. Sickness overwhelmed me once more and I hunched over my knees, waiting for the warm Mediterranean wind to blow the boat into port.

The rickety horse-drawn cart that carried me to my uncle's house forty miles away travelled quickly along the mountain roads. I stifled waves of nausea, my stomach yet to recover from the sea voyage. The driver was a frail old man with skin the colour of burnt umber who spoke just enough Turkish to understand that I needed to get to Amiandos, a village named after the neighbouring asbestos mine. I used the last of the money sent by my uncle to pay the driver and buy bread for the trip.

The old man showed no inclination to talk but he was a generous soul who offered me grapes and white cheese and black, shrunken olives. He knew every twist and turn in the road, every pothole and fresh spring where he would stop and let me drink sweet water. I watched him snooze in the seat of the carriage, the reins loosening in his hand, the obedient horse finding its own way along the steepening roads, pausing to munch on roadside bramble. As we ascended, I held my breath. The horse manoeuvred the wagon around hairpin bends, along precarious dust tracks that were danger- ously narrow. Afraid to look down, I focused instead on the vine-clad hills and the forests of evergreens that rose above me.

Rounding a corner at an altitude of 1500 feet, we came upon a stark moonscape. Vast swathes of the mountain resembled a polar desert, the bare plateaus devoid of natural life. This arid wasteland, spanning several hundred hectares, was crisscrossed by conveyor belts carrying hunks of rock to a large and noisy milling plant. Thousands of men worked the asbestos mine with pick axes, harvesting the valuable chrysotile veins within the lustrous rockface. The milling plant spewed out plumes of white powder that covered the men and machinery, coated the surrounding countryside with an ash-like patina.

I waved the old man goodbye on the path outside my uncle's house. A bearded man, with a white face and grey hair, answered the door. He cried out when he saw me and took me in his arms. I was embarrassed by the stranger's embrace, so tight and intimate, and stared into the small room, with its worn plaster walls and floor, searching for my uncle.

'Gabriel. It's me. Nareg. Don't you recognise me?' The man stood back, tears streaming down his face, leaving rivulets of pink flesh. He rubbed at his head, his face and his beard, clouding the air with white dust, revealing jet black hair and ruddy cheeks.

For three days, Nareg and his wife, Lena, celebrated my arrival, lighting the barbecue each night to feed Armenian friends and neighbours. I became living proof to all that miracles were possible, that a person could rise from the dead. If a nephew could materialise out of nowhere, after so many years, then so could a mother, a father or sister. They drank to my good health, praised God and savoured Nareg's meat. I was a passive spectator, unable to celebrate, to reciprocate Nareg's love, to embrace my new life in this harsh setting so unfamiliar and remote. At every opportunity I escaped the bustling house, the noise and the physical contact of strangers.

One day, I was sitting in the branches of a carob tree, hiding from the world, when I spotted Marta, feeding feral cats scraps of food and coaxing them into her lap. Dozens of scrawny creatures with matted hair appeared from bolt-holes like fugitives and rolled onto their backs, purring like generators when she touched them. I found myself wishing I were a cat being wooed and fed and stroked by this girl. As this thought crossed my mind, she looked up straight into my eyes and my cheeks flushed. It was a strange and disconcerting feeling. Marta didn't speak or dash away but continued to stroke the cats whose trust she had won with her gentleness. I waited until she had left before climbing down and making my way home but the next day, at the same time, I returned to the carob and hid once more in the leathery canopy. Marta came as I had hoped, beckoning the waifs with a click of her tongue and sat cross-legged to pet them.

In the weeks and months that followed, I grew accustomed to the pattern of life in the mountains. To the miners streaming to work at sunrise and Marta feeding the neighbourhood cats every afternoon, to the din of the mine and the all-pervasive dust that tinted the spring water flowing down the mountainside, covered the terracotta rooftops and settled on leaves. Dust that cloaked my uncle's hair and clothes, ageing him prematurely.

Every evening, my aunt Lena hung her husband's clothes on the washing line and beat out the grime with a broom, before sweeping the yard and hosing it down. The miners and their wives considered the dust innocuous, as harmless as the snowdrifts that covered the mountain in winter. They were too busy living hand to mouth to question why their fruit trees failed to thrive, why the miners suffered violent coughing fits in winter, why their chests felt heavy and why many men died before their time. The fresh mountain breeze, enjoyed in the village, was a mixed blessing, cooling the working miners while stoking up the earth and polluting the air with worm-like fibres that lodged tenaciously in the villagers' lungs.

Over time, my relationship with Nareg strengthened. He was a patient man and knew I needed time to heal. The boy who came to live with him bore little relation to the affectionate and confident nephew he had known in Caesaria. He struggled to connect with the sullen introvert I had become but he believed that love would eventually cure me, trigger my younger self into being.

He encouraged me to talk about the past. On our rambling walks, he listened and advised. In time, I unwound and the stories that haunted me poured out. I spoke about my father's execution, about life in the orphanage and Minas' fall from the clock tower, about the terror I had felt in the clearing. Nareg promised to leave the mountain as soon as he could and move to the capital where I would progress with my education. Every night, we lit a candle and placed it in the front window where it burned until daybreak. We were convinced that my mother was still alive and would one day appear on the doorstep with a child in her arms. The flickering halo in the window, that blackened the frame over time, was meant to lead Mama to the house if she arrived in the village late at night, when darkness was absolute.

Eighteen months after my arrival, I began to regard Nareg as a father and Amiandos as home. I loved Nareg with all my heart and, when he smiled, I recalled my mother's face. Nareg called me his miracle and, three years into my stay, a second miracle occurred. Lena had reached the fourth month of pregnancy after five years of unsuccessful attempts and several miscarriages.

I now took pleasure in the evening meal I shared with Nareg, Lena and the other Armenian friends who lived close by. Lena prepared simple dishes on a Primus stove in the corner of the room, mixing flour and water to make flat bread, stirring wheat *harissa* in a copper pan. Sitting at a table or standing if chairs ran out, Lena's guests shared bread, olives, cheese and thick-skinned yoghurt, recreating morsels of the life they had left behind. All considered Cyprus a safe place to wait before returning to their homes, to the fertile red earth their ancestors had farmed for thousands of years. At their nightly gatherings, the men chattered earnestly about the political situation in Turkey while the women recounted the horrors they had witnessed in 1915, weeping for relatives and friends they would never see again.

The long-awaited baby arrived a week prematurely and took the name of my grandmother, Varvar. Nareg returned to work the day after she was born while I looked after my aunt. I learned to cook, to help around the house, to beat the dust from uncle's clothes, while my aunt turned her attention to the baby. My connection to Varvar was instant as were my feelings of protectiveness and love. She was a reason to rejoice, swelling the ranks of our small clan, a fresh green shoot on a ravaged family tree.

The days leading up to her christening were busy and chaotic. Everyone in the village was invited, including the German managers who ran the mine. Lena and her neighbours spent several weeks preparing for the banquet, potting yoghurt and stuffing basturma sausages, distilling grape juice to make raki; pickling capers, milling wheat and spicing olives preserved in brine. The day before the christening, they baked bread and made paklava, layering filo pastry and filling it generously with sweetened nuts.

On the morning of the baptism, the mood in the village was festive. Nareg carried his daughter to the chapel on a slope above Amiandos while villagers followed on foot, riding horses or donkeys, wearing suits or pantaloons with polished leather boots. There were young men with fresh complexions, new to the mine, and rough-hewn old-timers whose hands and faces bore the scars of heavy labour, who looked awkward in rarely worn, starched white shirts.

Inside the chapel, Varvar was lowered into the font, enjoying the sensation at first before fright made her eyes widen and tiny fists tremble. As the priest daubed her face with oil, she scrunched up her pretty face to everyone's amusement. I hated hearing her cry but smiled with relief when she lunged at the priest and tugged at his cross.

The celebration began on our return to the village. Decorated tables and chairs lined the length of our street and several barbecues were already lit and manned by close friends, cooking pork, lamb and basturma. The smell of meat juices, garlic and cumin infused the mountainside, carried on curls of wood smoke, whetting our appetites. The men sipped raki and guzzled red wine, supplied by the Germans, while the women ferried heaving platters onto the tables: potatoes baked in a clay oven, sliced artichokes, bowls of salad with feta cheese, mounds of village bread and Lena's creamy yoghurt in earthenware pots.

I ate bread and basturma, sipped the raki my uncle said would put hairs on my chest, relishing the fiery taste and the feeling of mild intoxication. When the violinist began to play, I sprang to my feet and joined Nareg. Everyone clapped and chanted *dance Gabriel, dance*, and for the first time since Esther's wedding I set aside my inhibitions. The music took control of my body and I danced, arms raised, elbows jutting, crouching and leaping, hoping Marta was watching from the table where she sat with her parents, observing my exhibition of prowess, every joyful movement meant for her eyes only. Other men joined in and I stepped back, exhilarated, out of the circle that had formed.

I went in search of my young cousin, Varvar. She was grouchy and tired, unsettled by the noise, and I offered to take her for a walk. I carried her out of the village, to an orange grove where blossom had begun to pupate and she fell asleep in my arms. The distant thud of tumbling rock drew my attention and woke Varvar from her shallow sleep. I paid little attention to the crashing sound as I walked back to the village, thinking instead of Marta and how pretty she looked. I was accustomed to the mine's hum, to the sound of fragmenting rock, the rumble of machinery and intermittent explosions.

I expected to find the happy street scene I had left behind but instead I was shocked to see the women standing in a huddle, wailing and shouting. Lena was on her knees. A neighbour approached, relating garbled news ... the mine face had collapsed ... miners had been trapped beneath the rock ... the men had all gone to help. I handed Varvar to the neighbour and joined the women helping Lena to her feet. She threw her arms around my neck, repeating a mournful lament I was slow to register.

'He's dead, Gabriel. My husband is dead. Our Nareg is dead.'

I clung to my aunt to keep from collapsing. I remembered hearing rock fall and realised Varvar had woken up at the exact moment Nareg had perished beneath a landslide. My cousin screamed, opening her mouth wide and throwing back her head as if she knew she would grow up without a father.

Nareg had walked to the mine in high spirits, to take meat and wine to a group of working miners. Entering a hollow in the mountainside, where men worked with pickaxes, he had raised a toast to his daughter just as a ceiling of solid rock collapsed above him. He was crushed to death with five other men, including Marta's fifteen-year-old brother who was standing in for his father.

The widows and fatherless children returned to their empty homes. Neighbours and friends cleared away the evidence of merriment before visiting the bereaved to offer their condolences. The mining community was close knit and supportive but in the days that followed, I grew tired of the well-meaning women who took charge of Varvar, who brought food offerings several times a day and talked endlessly about Nareg's kindness and generosity, who listened to Lena voice her concerns, over and over again. How would she raise two children alone? How would she pay for my schooling? How would she find the emotional strength to attempt a life without her husband?

Two weeks after Nareg's death, I visited the mine and asked for a job. I was only fifteen but the German supervisor turned a blind eye to my age. I began work immediately, knowing I would never go to school or become a doctor, concentrating instead on supporting my aunt and my cousin. And every night after work, I lit two candles and set them on the windowsill, one to light my mother's way and the other for uncle Nareg's soul.

***

My audience is moved, especially Jennifer, who views me with moistened eyes. I light a cigarette, drained by the effort of excavating the depths of my memory. I have learned to recall the past with dispassion. A story told a thousand times over loses its drama, its punch, even when one's favourite uncle is the ill-fated protagonist.

'I think I should leave you to rest now, Mr Arakelian,' Jennifer says.

'Don't you want to hear the good bit?'

She is surprised by my flippancy. An anchoring sense of humour has helped me cope. 'My life hasn't all been a calamity. It was peppered with gifts and blessings. The most precious gift is sitting right here, beside me.' My wife's eyes mist over. 'After my uncle's death, I wandered the village like a sleepwalker, trying to ignore the pitiful looks. I was not the only aimless wanderer. Marta drifted too and our paths would cross in the fields and orchards outside the village. The sight of her made my young heart race and my skin tingle. I used to cover the bayonet scar on my face because I felt so self-conscious in her presence.'

Marta gently touches my cheek. 'The scar only added to your appeal.'

'Over time, I summoned the courage to look her in the eye and, one day, I waved and she waved back. That's when I knew she shared my feelings.'

'I felt sorry for you! You reminded me of a feral cat.'

'One day I stumbled across her on the path and we walked together in silence.'

'That was no coincidence. I was lying in wait.'

'Is that so? All these years, I never knew! We would meet at the carob tree in the orchard beyond the village, a ritual that lasted several years. In those days such behaviour was very risqué and would set the gossip mills churning.'

'We only held hands, Gabriel.'

'That was the highlight of my day until I turned eighteen and asked for your hand in marriage. Do you remember? Your father welcomed me into the family like a son. Marta became my life, my world. I loved the way she smiled, her gentle spirit and her elfin features. Our experience of loss, so sudden and traumatic, united us and binds us together to this day. The only beauty in that Godforsaken mountain was Marta. I never saw anything but ugliness in that mine.'

'Some saw its beauty,' Marta says. 'Do you remember the American photographer who came from National Geographic? The one who used you as his muse. I have a copy of the magazine somewhere.' She gets up to rummage through a bookcase drawer.

The photographer stayed in a stone house close to the mine for a week, where he developed his photos. Each well-judged shot encapsulated the malignancy of the mine, at odds with the beauty of its surroundings. The stark, white lunar landscape jarred with the vibrant green of the surrounding hills.

Marta finds the magazine, on its cover an angry young face with old man's eyes. A jaded miner with a defiant stare.

'Is that you, Mr Arakelian?' Jennifer asks.

'Yes. My unenviable claim to fame. It was that picture that strengthened my resolve to leave the mountain as soon as I could and forge a life I could feel proud of.'

Jennifer's eyes are clouded and dense. Then she smiles, thanks and embraces both of us. 'I think you need some rest, Mr Arakelian, but I hope you'll permit me to pay you another visit soon.'

Marta walks Jennifer to the door before returning to brush soft fingers through my thinning hair.

'I like that, Marta.'

'Lie back, Gabriel. Let me massage your head, my dear.'

She strokes my scalp with nimble fingers absorbing

pain twisted into the coils of my DNA, as ingrained as the colours that run through granite rock. I want to weep for the comfort of Marta's touch, a feeling so sublime and intense it makes me giddy.

Chapter 24

Katerina

Several days are taken up with visits to the mountain orchard and long, drawn-out meals in cosy taverns. Out-of-the-way places that serve wild mushrooms, cumin-infused sausages and cubes of barbecued, oregano lamb, everything washed down with red Troodos wine. I find myself hoping there's a heaven, that Gran is looking down with an approving eye.

One afternoon, we sit on the beach beneath an umbrella of woven grass, sharing a sun bed, and my thoughts return to Gran's story. I hand Ara the journal and he quickly finds the page where we left off, rereads. '*Rose found us, slumped at the base of a tree, hanging onto life by a thread.* Who was Rose?'

'The woman who adopted her. She was an American nurse who married an English teacher called Ernest. They settled in the Peak District in some remote farmhouse that belonged to Ernest's family. I only know them from pictures. They look quite austere but Gran said they were good people. They died a long time before I was born.'

Gran used to describe her life with Rose and Ernest as peaceful, a haven that nurtured her love of the countryside and rambling walks. The couple were in

129

their late thirties when they got married and Rose was ready for a quiet life after years spent tending the sick at mission schools in Turkey and the Middle East.

'Rose isn't the mystery. It's Levon. I don't know anything about him.'

'Perhaps they went their separate ways. Maybe he died from his wounds? The answer must lie somewhere in these pages.'

'That boy saved her life. He made her get up and walk. I'd hate to think she lost *him* too.'

Ara holds my gaze and moves his hand to mine. 'I don't want to lose *you*, Katerina. I don't want this to end. I can't stand the thought of you leaving.'

I can only think of reasons why I can't commit to this man, invest in a long-distance relationship bound to end.

'I don't see how this could work, Ara. I mean long-term.'

'The world's a small place.'

'I like *my* world. I'd be miserable without my family and friends and I've just been promoted to chief reporter. I need to focus on my work right now.'

'You could work here.'

'I really don't understand why we're having this conversation. We've only just met. Can't we just enjoy the now?'

I look away, to hide my uncertainty, and his hand falls limp in mine.

Chapter 25

Mariam, 1919

I was eleven years old, sitting on the backyard swing, lost in the past, remembering the street markets of Caesaria, watching Levon kicking a ball against a fence. He was tall and ungainly and looked older than twelve, especially when he was angry.

Four years had passed since Rose had found us in the forest on her way to Beirut. She had been working as a nurse at a mission school in the district of Bitlis, to the west of Lake Van, and was fleeing the troubles. She risked her life to ferry us to Lebanon, fought officialdom to keep us under her wing. We travelled to England, where Rose had relatives, where she met and married Ernest, a teacher. They settled in a cottage in the Peak District, Ernest's family home. Rose referred to the cottage as a sanctuary where we could all heal. She shunned the outside world, avoiding newspapers and the radio. Ernest's sister, Irene, came to visit with her family twice a year but there were no other regular visitors. Rose was worn out after her experiences abroad and needed a quiet retreat away from the world. She wrestled with demons, she told us, with indelible images of the children she had failed to protect but she wouldn't elaborate and this only made sense to us later, when we happened across a document she never meant for us to see.

We lived frugally and were largely self-sufficient. Rose made her own bread and cheese, and sewed simple cotton clothes for the four of us. She taught me to knit and I found the repetitious action of hooking and flicking the needles soothing, an escape from my thoughts. We kept hens, rabbits and a goat and a neighbouring farmer supplied us with milk and flour. Ernest grew vegetables and was handy around the house: he taught himself basic carpentry. The nearest village, with its grocery shop, post office and parish church, was a thirty-minute drive in the horse and trap. We shopped for supplies once a month and were allowed to buy sweets and chocolate. Most Sundays we attended church where Levon and I felt like outsiders, dark-skinned oddities in ill-fitting homespun garments.

The cottage stood alone at the end of a long, deserted road, nestled in acres of rolling farmland. Levon hated the silence and hankered after the clatter of neighbours and street hawkers. There was nothing familiar in our surroundings, no reminders of home whatsoever. We had been dropped into a moonscape of green where clouds billowed overhead and winter winds cut to the bone. Levon was my only link to the past in this alien landscape. With him I could let off steam and speak my mother tongue. He could read my mind, tune into my feelings, and bring me back to life when I felt miserable and apathetic. My thoughts often returned to the clearing and my brothers, the memory of their burial place, a bone-strewn graveyard where young boys' skulls lay grimacing.

We had both given Rose a list of names, friends and relations who might still be alive. My list included my mother, Nvart, Lousine and Esther, everyone whose death I had not directly witnessed. Rose had sent these names to her friend, Elsie Barrow. They had worked together at the mission school in Bitlis and now Elsie was a Red Cross volunteer in New York, helping refugees trace missing relatives. Every day we lit candles for our mothers and friends and prayed they would be found but, as the years passed, my hopes faded, while Levon continued to believe in miracles.

Levon smashed the ball against the fence, venting his frustration on the wooden posts. He often raged against the injustice we had suffered, stomping through the quiet house like a wounded bear. Everyday Levon raked up the past, shared the stories of his childhood, refusing to let go of our old lives, embrace the new. He preferred to remember while I just wanted to forget, pretend the past had never happened.

'Mariam!' Levon called me over, staring at something on the ground. I walked across a lawn of stubby grass to find him standing over a dead sparrow, a mash of pink innards spewing from its chest. 'It must have been killed by a cat. Shall we bury it?'

I had grown used to Levon's fascination with death and burials. The back yard was littered with makeshift crosses marking the graves of the lifeless creatures we had come across.

133

He dug a hole with his hands in the flowerbed and buried the bird. Then we stood over the grave, crossing ourselves and mumbling sombre prayers.

Rose knocked on the kitchen window and called us inside for our lessons and Levon whined all the way to the back door. We were home-schooled and began each day with a short reading from the Bible. Rose's parents were missionaries but she didn't share their religious zeal. In our house, more emphasis was placed on the teaching of history, geography, arithmetic and penmanship. There were plenty of Ernest's old books scattered around and in our free time we were encouraged to read: Dickens, Mark Twain, Rudyard Kipling, Aesop's Fables, the poetry of Emily Dickinson and Robert Louis Stevenson. Levon had no interest in books, preferring to help Rose in the kitchen or Ernest in his workshop, finding solace in physical labour.

We took our seats, Levon sprawling forward on the table, his head resting on his arm.

'Sit up, Levon,' Rose said.

He promptly sat back, slouched in his chair.

'Mariam, would you read your favourite verse from Jeremiah?' she said.

I flicked through the pages, found the passage I was looking for, one that gave me hope for the future. '*For I know the plans I have for you, declares the Lord, plans to prosper you and not to harm you, plans to give you hope and future. Then you will call upon me and I will listen . . .*'

I enjoyed reading aloud from the Bible, believing in the power of prayer, and found the stories gripping and invigorating.

When I had finished, Rose asked Levon to read. He sucked air through his teeth before reaching for the Bible, thumbing through the pages, stopping arbitrarily. He began, mispronouncing words, ignoring punctuation, hurrying along carelessly. Nothing in the Bible stirred Levon or captured his imagination; not the Creation or the Fall, not the Book of Matthew or the stories of struggle and sacrifice that mirrored our own experience.

'I don't want to do this.' He scraped back his chair, biting his lip.

'One more try, Levon,' Rose said, a slight shrill in her voice, patience wearing thin.

'No.'

'Then you'll go straight to your room and stay there.' Her sour tone made little impression on Levon.

He stood up, bunching long arms across his chest. 'You can't tell me what to do. You're not my mother.' This was not the first time he had denied her maternal rights, reminding her of the women whose memory overarched our lives.

'I'm the only mother you have so you'd better listen to me or else.'

'Or else what?' He leapt from his chair muttering curses in Armenian and stormed out of the kitchen.

'You'd better go after him, Mariam,' Rose said, afraid of what he might do when gripped by sudden rage.

I followed him into the yard, tuned into his angry rhetoric. 'I don't want to read the Bible or speak English. I want to speak our language, be myself.'

We had reached the thicket of trees beyond the

backyard and Levon wove through a dense coppice. We often played in the woods overlooking the cottage. Rose encouraged us to play outside, to explore the landscape of our new country and use up our energies walking, climbing trees, helping Ernest in the garden. After our lessons, we could do as we pleased, for Rose believed that freedom would aid our recovery, lessen the nightmares.

We reached our favourite tree, a sprawling chestnut, and Levon made a foothold with his hands. I hauled myself up and soon we were perched on a thick branch, our legs swinging several metres above ground, hidden from view.

'We mustn't forget who we are and where we come from,' he said. 'Who wants to be English, anyway? They don't dance with their arms in the air or sing the way we do. They don't cry when they're happy or shout when they talk and they don't know how to eat. I can't bear another mouthful of Rose's terrible cheese, another tasteless bowl of oats. Dear God, please let me have one more taste of my mother's sheep's head stew before I die.'

My mouth watered at the thought of the delicacy cooked on feast days.

'Can you imagine what Rose would say if I asked her to boil a sheep's head? She'd think I'd proposed some satanic ritual. She already thinks I'm the antichrist.' He sucked air through his teeth. 'I miss my mother's cooking, don't you, Mariam? Do you remember crunching open fresh almonds, the flavour of sweet melons? What I'd give for one bite of my mother's lahmajoon.'

He cried theatrically and laid his head on my shoulder. I loved the way Levon enthused about food, his garrulousness. I knew he would never find peace at the cottage where life lacked the excitement and colour, the company he craved, the foods he yearned for. His soul was restless and set for adventure and I feared this place would not contain him for long.

I wore a flowery dress with a high collar, buttoned to the nape. Stood beside Levon at the back of the church, singing The Lord's My Shepherd. The choir was tuneful but didn't move me like the haunting voices in the church of St Gregory. The parish church was white-walled and bare, with an altar table at one end and a stone font at the other. There were wooden benches, a simple metal cross above the pulpit and a scattering of half-molten candles.

From the corner of my eye, I could see Levon's lips moving in time to the hymn but he made no sound. He never sang in church, but would put on quite a show, opening his mouth wide like a hungry bird. I knew Rose would have words with him later for playing the fool in God's house.

When the service ended, Rose and Ernest mingled with the few friends they had made in the parish. A small, blonde girl turned to stare at us, pulled at her mother's skirt and pointed. The woman gave us a compassionate smile and then I heard the word *orphans* and felt I had been stabbed in the heart.

'Did you hear that?' Levon said, glaring at the girl who buried her head in her mother's skirts.

'She didn't mean anything by it.'

'We're not orphans,' he said. 'Our mothers are alive. I know they are, and one day they'll find us.'

We played Twenty-One for sweets, sitting in the attic. I dealt Levon a card hoping I would win for a change. He usually beat me and spent the entire game sucking caramel or chewing marshmallows.

He played cards once a week with the farmer's son, Stewart, who lived on the neighbouring plot, setting out with a supply of chocolates and caramels which he gambled, returning with pockets bulging with coins and extra sweets. Levon was saving his winnings to fund his escape from the village, if his worst fears were realised and noone came to claim us.

I turned my cards face up and dealt a ten of hearts. Levon had won, again. 'More sweets for me,' he said, pulling the bag towards him and drawing out a stick of liquorice.

I threw down the deck. 'You always win. It's not fair.'

'I've always been good at games. I take after my father.' He stopped munching, the sweet seeming to stick in his throat. 'The older I get the more I look like him, the more I feel that he's inside me.' Levon's eyes told me he was back in his village, with a father who was marched from home at gunpoint, accused of treason. When the police came to round up more men, Levon fled the village, joined a caravan of exiles and was separated from his family. 'Do you think the spirit lives forever, Mariam?'

I wanted to believe that the essence of the people we

had lost lived on. He drew closer and handed over the sweets. 'Let's eat until we burst. Until our stomachs hurt and our teeth rot.'

I was taken back in time to Esther's wedding, the day Gabriel and I nibbled halva beneath the pear tree. Levon's elaborate gestures and excitability often brought Gabriel to mind.

The smell of wood smoke rose into the attic from the hearth below. The dark roof space was strewn with trunks and wooden boxes, lit by an oil lamp and several candles. I sat on an old wicker chair and Levon on a seat he had fashioned from a tree trunk in Ernest's workshop. We used a suitcase as a table and had sneaked away household objects to make our den more homely: teacups, vases, a blanket and rug. I kept my knitting needles in the attic and had made myself a doll, as well as a colourful cushion for Levon. We had gathered a few games and paper for sketching. Beside my chair, I kept a small pile of weathered pamphlets, books and journals: several dog-eared copies of Sajous' Medical Journal and a clutch of Red Cross First Aid manuals, a small library Rose had used for her medical training before setting off on her travels. In a corner, beneath the window, was our altar, set with candles, where we prayed for our mothers' return.

'I'm in the mood for a story,' Levon said. 'One of those your brother used to tell.'

'You've heard them all a thousand times.'

Levon never tired of legends about sun maidens and fire spirits, invincible roosters and mysterious snake children. I had almost exhausted Gabriel's repertoire but there was one I hadn't told, a story that brought back memories of lying beside Gabriel in the wilderness. I still longed for my brothers though the contours of their faces were blurred in my memory, charcoal drawings smudged by the finger of time.

I relayed the story of the Seven Stars about the boy and girl who fell in love but weren't allowed to marry, the couple who died of broken hearts and rose to heaven becoming stars. Levon had paper on his lap and sketched two children rising into the sky, holding hands. He liked to draw and could sit for hours conjuring the characters from my stories. The girl had long wavy hair like mine and the boy had a skewed smile and large ears, Levon's caricature of himself. I thought it strange that he had drawn us together in this way, fingers laced as if we were a couple.

When I had finished the story, I felt a longing for home. The fairy tale released a flood of memories and set me thinking about the afterlife. I wondered if people aged in heaven. Would Gabriel be a curlyhaired boy with a toothy smile for all eternity? If heaven were as big as England, how would I ever find him? And how would my mother find me set adrift in an ocean of green? Our situation seemed hopeless.

'What are you thinking about?' Levon asked.

'My mother.'

'She'll appear soon enough. Take you away from here.'

'What about Rose and Ernest?' I had come to love the people who had adopted us and the cottage had become my home.

'They're not our parents. You mustn't forget that.'

Levon had shut Rose and Ernest out of his heart, as if loving them was a betrayal of his birth parents. I often thought about my mother but the aching had eased and when Rose squeezed me in her arms I felt every bit her daughter.

'We'll never return home, Levon. Why don't you just accept it?'

'We can go there right now, if you want.'

'What are you talking about?'

'Up here, we can be wherever we want.' He blew out the candles and extinguished the oil lamp, casting the attic into darkness. 'Where would you like to be right now, Mariam?'

'In the drawing room of my home in Caesaria.'

'And who would you like to be here?'

'My father.'

'He's right here. Can't you see him? Who else?'

'Baba's friend, the poet Badalian.'

'He's just arrived. He's taking off his overcoat. It's a very well-made coat, lined with silk.'

'The poet's coat was shabby. I don't think he cared about clothes.'

'He's come up in the world. He's a famous man now, a published poet. He can afford silk.'

'And where's my father standing?'

'Right in front of you, smoking a pipe. Can't you smell the smoke? It's so pungent I can barely breathe. And who am I?'

'You're the lawyer, Carabetian, and you've come for tea.'

141

I embraced the darkness, filling it with the people I missed, imagining I could see my father's outline, the proud curve of his back, the gleam of his hair oil.

'Where's my tea?' Levon asked.

I rattled a teacup in its saucer, gave it a stir. 'Here it is, sweetened with a spoonful of honey.'

Levon made a slurping sound. 'It's truly delicious, little flower. How about one of your pastries? I'm feeling rather peckish.'

I loved this game and hearing my pet name made me happy.

'Here. Take one, fresh from the oven.' I swear I caught a whiff of my mother's pastries made with mint and cheese. I was back in Caesaria with the snowy peaks of Mount Erciyes glistening beyond the imaginary window.

Levon chomped, slurped and rolled appreciative sounds. 'Mmm. Delicious. I have never tasted better. I will certainly come here again, though the lighting is a little subdued for my liking.'

I smiled.

'I can see you smiling,' he said.

'How do you know I'm smiling?'

'I can see in the dark.'

'Then what am I doing now?' I stuck out my tongue.

'You're ... rolling your eyes ... pulling a face ... sticking out your tongue?'

My smile faded as the spectral vision of my father blurred, dissolved into black and I was suddenly back in the attic feeling bereft.

'I never told you what happened to my father's friends.'

'Tell me.'

'The lawyer had the soles of his feet sliced off and the poet had his tongue cut out.' I shuddered and the darkness began closing in. 'Levon, are you still there?'

He sensed my panic and reached for my hand. 'I'm here, Mariam. Don't be afraid.'

Levon struck a match and lit a candle, extinguishing the past.

I lay in the back yard, nimbus clouds billowing overhead. Beside me, Levon hummed a tune while I chewed flavourless gum, imagining it was halva.

'I'd give anything for a piece of halva.' I voiced my thoughts and Levon stirred onto his elbow.

'Why don't we make some?'

'I wouldn't know where to start.'

'We'll make it up as we go along. How complicated can it be? Come on. Rose and Ernest won't be back for hours and the stove's still hot from breakfast.'

Carried away by his enthusiasm, I followed Levon into the kitchen and watched him grab a bag of sugar from the pantry and pour it into a pan on the stove. He added water, stirring with a wooden spoon.

'It needs to be soft and chewy,' he said. 'Sugar and water won't do the job. We need to add something else.'

'Like what?'

He looked thoughtful and then his eyes widened. 'Go up into the attic and fetch me a bag of marshmallows and anything else you like the taste of.'

I soon returned, armed with marshmallows and a box of assorted chocolates. Levon poured the confections into the pan and a syrupy aroma filled the kitchen, whetting my appetite. Then he tossed the chocolates in, one by one, stirring until all the ingredients had melted in stringy, creamy whirls, before pouring the mixture into a metal dish.

We carried the cooling tray into the attic, played cards until the sweet had set. Levon cut it into squares and offered me the first piece. I took a bite, chewed on a concoction that was soft and chewy, raspingly sweet, shot through with chocolate and caramel.

'This stuff is good enough to sell,' he said. 'That's how I'll make my fortune. Selling halva. We'll share the profits, then we'll both be rich.'

Levon had fancy dreams and I loved to hear them, to travel to a future where we lived together in a big house and ran our own restaurant. I had no dreams of my own and was happy to adopt Levon's vision, to imagine the grand life we would live together as recompense for everything we had lost.

He began rooting through the trunks in the attics, a favourite pastime, one that yielded Ernest's childhood toys and family hand-me-downs: pictures, trinkets, books, patchwork quilts.

That day, Levon forced open a hidden drawer in one of the trunks and found a clutch of typewritten papers, a sworn statement made by Rose in 1918 for the *American Board of Commissioners for Foreign Affairs* detailing her experiences at the Mission school in Bitlis where she had nursed children with Typhus. That day we learned about the bravery of a woman who risked her safety to hide exiled Armenians in the basement of the school, who had grown to love the orphans left at the gate by fleeing mothers and was left heartbroken when the students were marched away at gunpoint. She wrote of her escape from the region, aided by the school's Turkish caretaker, and the sights she witnessed on the carriage journey to Beirut –the sea of exiles, frightened and resigned to death. She described the moment she found us, bloodied and in rags, and her determination to protect us come what may, calling us her gift from God.

Chapter 26

Katerina

One question absorbs me. What happened to Levon? How did he disappear so completely from the landscape of my grandmother's life? What happened to the boy who shared a key part of her childhood? I wait for Ara to arrive, try to focus on reading a novel but I'm a hive of contradictory emotions: a clenching sadness for Gran, confusion about my own future and my feelings for Ara. A warm flush seeps through me as I dwell on the last few days. Perhaps it could work from afar on a trial basis, maybe we were destined to meet, assisted by Gran's spirit.

I glance at my watch, anticipating his arrival. An hour passes, then two. He'll arrive, I tell myself, because he promised he would and a final chapter remains. Last night, on the beach, he unveiled his feelings. I ring the workshop and his flat from reception but there's no answer so I walk along the seafront, an argument raging in my head, oscillating between heart and reason. Is this the Rob saga all over again, a case of Katerina slipping into romantic foolery and reading too much into empty words? I seek solace in ice cream, two scoops of pistachio, and sit watching the sea, feeling rejected. I long to know why he hasn't come, wonder if he's sick but I'm too proud to call again or pay him a visit and I tell myself his disappearance is probably for the best.

Back at the hotel, Jenny's sitting on her bed, nibbling a slab of chocolate.

'It's over,' she says, with a dismissive shrug, referring to her week of casual pleasure. My friend is armour-plated and won't lose sleep over a holiday fling.

'That makes two of us.'

'Now, that *is* a surprise. You OK?' She sees through the smile, her concern making my eyes sting.

We resume our old habits the following day, getting up late, eating fast food, lying on the beach for hours before heading to the Irish bar until the early hours. On the penultimate day of our fortnight's break, I start transcribing Ara's recordings and hearing his voice again fills me with righteous anger that needs a vent. He offered to translate the journal and left behind loose ends, betraying our friendship. I decide to have it out with him, before I go home. After all, I'll never see him again. I find myself fixing my hair the way he likes it, swept to one side, and head for the workshop, churning satisfying insults to hurl.

A sculpture catches my eye in the café, close to the workshop, and I stop to take a look. It's Ara's Cycladic nude taking pride of place in the window and then I see its maker sitting with his back to me at a table with a group of creative types, leisurely smoking and supping coffee. I head away, the anger returning, the truth now utterly apparent. He has returned to a life on a different track and the only thing that bound us was my grand-mother's past.

Chapter 27

Gabriel

'I understand your problem, my friend.' Hovsepian says, our conversation whispered in a quiet corner of the club.

'Marta has invited Harry's parents over for dinner on Sunday. In-laws, she calls them, *khenami*. Over my dead body! I have been warned to be on my best behaviour or else.'

'Or else what?'

'Or else I will never enjoy another plate of baked lamb as long as I live, never sink my teeth into a cheese turnover, never again be treated to the delight of a head massage.'

'You have let your wife rule the roost for too long, my friend.'

'Let's change the subject, Partogh's coming over.'

'What are you two whispering about?' Partogh asks.

'If we wanted you to know we wouldn't be whispering,' Hovsepian says.

'How's your *khenami*, Gabriel?'

'Bite your tongue, Partogh.'

'What do you have against the boy? He seems perfectly decent to me.'

'Where do you want me to start? His tight clothes, scarecrow hair . . . '

149

'The clothes of the young are meant to offend old sticks like us. It's all about the new generation disassociating itself, just as it should, making its own mark in the world.'

'My son-in-law doesn't dress like that,' Hovsepian says.

'Your son-in-law wears the jumpers his mother knits.'

Standing on the top rung of my ladder, I peer into the bird's nest in the carob tree. Four glossy, blue eggs lie in the cup-shaped nest. I hear Marta calling out my name and see her exit through the back door and tickle a feral cat under the chin. Viewing her secretly, I am reminded of the day I first saw her and my old heart misses a beat I am a boy again, spying on the girl I love, wishing I were a cat.

She walks towards the tree, stands beneath it, looking for me. I pull off a carob and drop it on her head. Her hands move to her hips.

'What in God's name are you doing up there, Gabriel?'

'I was checking on the birds' eggs. Making sure the snake hasn't got to them.'

'Come down before you break a leg. That old ladder is a health hazard.'

I do as I'm told and head back to my glass of whisky on the garden table.

'Do you know your problem, Gabriel? You have too much time on your hands,' Marta says. 'You need to find more work. Be proactive, market yourself. Anahit would love it if you took the photos at her wedding.

It would give you something to do. Keep you out of trouble.'

I made a name for myself as a photographer in the forties and fifties. Everyone sought to have their weddings and christenings snapped by Gabriel Arakelian. These days, I work sporadically, as a favour for friends, the loss of my home and my shop sapping my interest in a profession I grew to love.

'There's not going to be a wedding. She's not marrying that half-wit.'

Marta sighs and marches back into the house. Photos indeed. Every shot would feel like salting a wound. A movement catches my eye beyond the fence, beneath the tangle of dry vegetation. I wonder if Therko is staking out the yard, peering at me through the undergrowth, waiting for his chance to grasp at those eggs. Something must be done to halt these audacious daytime advances. I rack my brain for a solution. I could borrow Hovsepian's hunting rifle and shoot the blighter or buy a trap. With a car battery and a few lengths of wire I could electrify the fence to keep the intruder off my premises round the clock. I decide to visit my old friend Pavlos, the local mechanic, with a bottle of Partogh's homemade raki in exchange for a car battery.

It is Sunday. Marta has strung the backyard with lights, set a table for six beneath the carob tree, laid out her best china and borrowed crystal glasses from the neighbour. I sit and watch her tweaking the napkins into peaks, drowning my contempt with whisky, limbering up for my performance. I must make my hostility plain without seeming outwardly rude and risking dietary hardship.

Marta has pushed out the culinary boat, squandering a week's grocery budget. The table is teeming with sumptuous dishes. Harry's taxi driver father, Jakovos, sits opposite, beside his wife, Rina. I fill my mouth with soft lamb flavoured with garlic, pepper and rosemary, savour the taste like a man soon to be starved for some minor social infringement.

Jakovos is everything I expect him to be, one of the great unwashed. He has the prerequisite taxi driver stomach and moustache and, if I am not mistaken, he is wearing a hairpiece made of tufty, acrylic strands. I wonder what my granddaughter thinks he and I will spend Sunday afternoons discussing. Wheel hubs and spark plugs? Engine oil and catalytic converters? I would rather boil my own head.

He has a loud, raucous laugh, throwing back his head to guffaw at his own crude, cabby jokes, one about two dumb blondes stuck down a well and another about a Pontian Greek who tries to rob a bank with a banana. If he dares tell a joke about the miserly Armenian, I shall plant his face in the yoghurt dip. Marta's intermittent glares are phenomenally unjust. She can't possibly expect me to laugh at jokes that are discriminatory, unsophisticated and inherently unfunny.

Harry's mother is as plump as a custard-filled pastry and has nothing of Marta's physical delicacy. Her ankles are thick and her swollen fingers festooned with garish gold rings. She spends a considerable amount of time describing the trouble she is having with her peptic ulcer. *I have no appetite,* she says, spooning a second helping of pilaf onto her plate. *I really shouldn't eat,* she says, taking the last piece of lamb shoulder, gulping away a considerable portion of my pension with a pained expression that is hardly convincing.

Anahit raises her brows, hooking my face with her stare, and I struggle, really I do, to think of something to say. Something stimulating, something that will please Marta and my granddaughter. The plate of artichoke hearts shimmering in their dressing of oil and lemon gives me an idea.

'What is your opinion on cardiac transplantation?' I ask the taxi driver.

'Come again?' he says.

'Heart transplants. Did you hear about the baby girl in America born with a severe heart defect? Doctors sewed a walnut-sized baboon heart into her tiny chest. She lived three weeks on a simian organ.'

'What was the point of that?'

'The point!' The ass. 'The transplant worked. It was a medical miracle opening the road to cross-species transplantation.'

'I wouldn't want a monkey heart in my chest.'

'Even if you were suffering from severe coronary disease and were given days to live?'

'I will go to my maker just as I am.'

'Your family might feel differently.' I turn to Rina who has finally placed her fork beside her knife on the empty plate. 'If your husband was suffering from end-stage heart failure, wouldn't you want him to have a transplant?'

153

'I don't like to think about it.'

'If he was at the edge of a river being chased by lions, wouldn't you push him in?'

'He can't swim.'

'I was being metaphorical, woman! Surely you must have an opinion on the most extraordinary milestone in the field of life-extending surgery.'

'Stop hollering.' Anahit says.

Harry's mother looks cowed, slightly yellow, and I wonder if her liver is playing up as well as her ulcer.

'My grandfather has a keen interest in medicine,' Anahit says, with an apologetic smile. 'His father, Grigor, was a doctor.'

'Did I tell you the joke about the man without a heart,' the taxi driver says.

'No, Papa. And we don't want to hear it,' Harry says.

'Gabriel, perhaps we should change the subject.'

'What would you like me to talk about, Marta, hubcaps, furry dice?'

'Have you dealt with the snake yet, Mr Arakelian?' Harry asks.

'No, but I've set up a trap.' I point to an overturned box in the corner, propped up by a twig bound with string, a rudimentary mousetrap.

'What snake?' Rina says, clapping a hand on her heart.

'The snake that lives in the branches of this carob when it is not slithering around the back yard being a nuisance.'

Rina crosses herself and looks up with a shiver. 'I hate snakes. Just the thought of them makes my skin crawl.'

'Let's talk about something more pleasant,' Marta says.

Rina claps her fleshy hands together. 'Yes. Like weddings. My son's will be the biggest and best this city has ever known.'

'And who is the lucky girl?' My quip meets with glares all round.

'My grandfather's joking. That's his way,' Anahit says. 'He can't help himself.'

'I wish that were true. I think this whole thing is a rushed state of affairs and I don't understand why.'

'They've been dating for five years,' the taxi driver says.

'And if I had my way they'd date for five more.'

'Why? Isn't my son good enough for your granddaughter?'

'My granddaughter is an educated girl, a teacher, and your son is . . .'

Before I have finished my sentence the Neanderthal has pushed back his chair and is ordering his wife out of her seat. He heads for the back door, muttering curses under his breath and my family follow him, throwing me angry looks. I don't feel a smattering of remorse until later that day when Anahit packs a suitcase, announcing she is moving in with Harry.

My normally measured wife hisses at me. 'Are you happy about your granddaughter leaving? We promised her parents we'd take good care of her. Tonight, Gabriel Arakelian, you will be sleeping with your snake.'

That night she locks me out of the house.

Chapter 28

Jennifer comes back the following Wednesday at Marta's invitation, stepping into the house with a disconcertingly warm air, kissing my cheeks. I am not one for slobbery kisses and the feeling of her greasy lipstick on my skin is vaguely repellent. I have insulted her hairstyle and still she has warmed to me unless this show of affection is the American way to win my confidence and draw me out. The boundaries of our relationship are clear enough to me – she is the interviewer and I am the interviewee.

The smell of freshly cooked pastries wafts through the house. Marta has been busy in the kitchen, making *banir boregs*, cheese turnovers. She comes into the room, wiping flour-dusted hands on her apron, greeting Jennifer with kisses. I can't remember the last time Marta kissed me.

Before long, we are all sitting at the dining table, drinking tea and munching turnovers, the women chatting merrily about nothing as only they can. I help myself to a second turnover and Marta throws me a glance like the flick of a forked tongue, a glance that says in a low, warning voice, *Gabriel, take another pastry and I will cut off your hand. Remember you have high cholesterol, angina and a pot belly. Remember that I recently had to let out the waistband on your favourite trousers and next time this need arises, I will carry out my threat and dispose of the garment.*

The glance has a point but I eat the pastry anyway, knowing it will be my last for some time.

'Shall we begin, Mr Arakelian?' Jennifer asks. 'Last time, you spoke about your life in the mountains. It might be easier to go chronologically.'

Today my thoughts are a jumbled mass and I need whisky to order them. 'Just a moment.'

'Oh, Gabriel. You're wasting Jennifer's time. She has other people to interview.'

'Don't worry about my time. I'm happy for Mr Arakelian to take things at his own pace.'

I go to the kitchen and pour myself a Johnny Walker from the fridge, filling the glass to the rim, looking forward to its mellowing influence. There is always a bottle or two of premium scotch in the house, giving off a fruity, medicinal scent. Marta waters down my whisky, obliging me to drink double the quantity. I keep a small flask of unadulterated spirit in my wardrobe and take a swig at bedtime whenever I feel agitated, when dreams swamp me in a cold sweat. Nightmares in which Marta is carted away by a masked horseman, Tamar is dressed in rags, begging for food, and Anahit lies dying. If the jitters will not subside with whisky, I turn to my secret stash of Ativan, a sedative that helps me sleep. In this country, most prescription drugs can be bought over-the-counter if you know the right pharmacist.

I catch sight of my ageing reflection in the hallway

mirror as I walk back to the room. My skin is grooved like an intricate origami puzzle, unfolded and set down across the contours of my bony face. My boomerang mouth makes me appear perpetually vexed, even on the rare occasion when I am happy, when Tamar comes to visit, when grandchildren fill the house. A faint scar runs along my right cheek, my branding, proof, if it were needed, of that day in the clearing when I lost my brother and sister.

Marta watches me return to my place at the table, the intensity of her stare making me spill amber drops on the tiled floor.

'That was your fault,' I say, pre-empting a lecture on the stupidity of filling my glass to the rim.

I take a healthy slurp to prevent further spillage, and reach for my Rothmans.

'Did you ever find out what happened to your mother, Mr Arakelian?'

'I wrote to every Armenian parish in the world. I searched through records. I even hired a private detective.'

'A detective! Won't you tell me about that?'

'He was Lebanese. His name was Farid. I remember the exact day he came to me with news. It was on the King's birthday, a day I would face great disappointment and great joy. That has been the general pattern of my life, Jennifer . . . '

Chapter 29

Nicosia, 1937

I sat on the balcony of our tenement in the capital, watching the neighbourhood come to life. My camera was ready, fitted with a new reel of film. A freelance photographer, I had been hired by a newspaper to take pictures of the King's birthday celebrations on the parade ground, a short walk from the tenement.

I had moved my family from the mountain several years earlier, to Nicosia's Turkish quarter where the Armenian community was well-established and thriving. I lived with a gaggle of women: with Marta and my young daughter Tamar, with my aunt Lena and cousin Varvar. The women had settled well into city life, had made numerous friends and often drank coffee with our Turkish neighbour Begum. She was a generous soul, who always came round on feast days and birthdays bringing flour halva, almond cookies and semolina pudding. She reminded me of Esra, the woman who had saved my life and often came to me in waking dreams, an ageless presence in a fringed headscarf. I wondered what had become of her, wished I had been given the chance to say goodbye and express my gratitude.

Marta and Lena shopped at Armenian and Turkish

stalls and shops where many of the foods we had craved could be found: basturma sausages, thick creamy yoghurt set in ceramic pots, fragrant teas, halva and nuts rolled in burnt sugar. I had no regrets about leaving the drudgery of the mine and escaping old haunts that reminded me of my uncle. We turned a blind eye to pockets of violence in the city, to political unrest fuelled by Greek Cypriot opposition to British rule.

For the first six months I had taken any work that came my way until old Bedros, the Armenian photographer, offered me an apprenticeship. I was enthralled with the Kodak he thrust into my hands and regarded my new job as a satisfying compromise, halfway between the non-manual life of the suited gentleman I coveted and the physical graft of the common labourer. People were always pleased to see me, wanting their images immortalised, their rites of passage recorded for posterity: christenings, betrothals, marriages. Photographs endured, surviving oppression, tyranny and massacre. Many Armenian friends had fled their homes in 1915 clutching only family pictures. The image of my father framed on the mantel was my most treasured possession, the one thing I would save if all else were lost. I wished I had more pictures of my family, that I had taken photos instead of bread on the day we were forced from our home.

My job was poorly paid and I was forced to spend the money I had saved while working at the mine. I carried the last of that money in my pocket to pay the man I had arranged to meet at Ahmet's coffee house, the Lebanese agent Farid, who specialised in tracking down lost Armenian relatives. Farid had sent news, through the club, that he had information about my mother. The passage of time had not dulled my hope of finding her because I felt her life force urging me to continue my search. She was out there, somewhere in the world, and no one could convince me otherwise.

I set out for the meeting on foot through a quarter scarred by past battles. There were ruined churches and fragments of arches, ornate doorways that led nowhere, weathered frescoes on crumbling walls. Chilling evidence of tyranny was everywhere in the landscape, from the Venetian battlements erected in the 16th century to fortify the city against Ottoman attack, to the flat-roofed houses with small windows, built to provide security against invasion and persecution from the island's despotic rulers. A whole raft of conquerors had stamped their mark: Egyptians, Persians, Lusignans, Turks, with Cyprus becoming a Crown colony in 1925 following the demise of the Ottoman Empire. The island was sold and bartered at the will of foreign nations with strategic and territorial interests. I sensed that trouble would one day revisit this place so pockmarked by a turbulent history.

Luckily, I had missed the riots of 1931 when anti-British protestors, inflamed by chants of *Down with the tyrants!* And *Out with the foreigners!* had stormed Government House, smashing glass and setting the place alight. A brick narrowly missed the British governor, Ronald Storrs, who jumped from his bed and ran for his life. Government House was burned to the ground while protestors looked on, cheering and singing the

Greek national anthem. In the coming days, the British army had made its presence felt in the capital, and a state of emergency was announced.

Just beyond the Venetian gate, I entered Ahmet's coffee house, crowded with customers and thick with pungent smoke. The name of the owner was printed in bold lettering on a dusty canvas awning, riddled with holes through which beams of sunlight stretched like spectral fingers. Men in white pantaloons sucked on water pipes while others puffed cigarettes and rolled dice. These men seemed to have unlimited time for idleness on their hands, an indolence about them I would never come to understand. The café was popular with Turks and Armenians, many of whom were close friends. We were used to living together, comfortable companions in spite of our history, sharing a common language. Some Armenians could barely speak a word of Greek but conversed easily in Turkish, the language of the homeland.

Farid sat at the far end of the coffee house. He greeted me with the ingratiating smile of a man who would soon be lining his pockets. I gave him the envelope filled with cash and his smile widened.

'How are you, my friend?' he asked.

'What news have you brought me, Farid?' I wanted news about my mother, not small talk.

'Let me buy you a drink, Mr Arakelian.'

My stomach churned in anticipation. 'Just tell me what you know.'

'I found a woman who met your mother at Katma, several weeks after you were separated.'

My heart pounded. My mother reached Katma, survived the worst part of the journey and there was every hope she was still alive, lived and breathed in another part of the world. I knew of Katma – we all did. It was a notorious transit camp for refugees, a narrow strip of desert surrounded by barren hills, the gateway to Aleppo, a stopping off point or final resting place. I had heard first-hand reports about the conditions at Katma, about the stench of human refuse and rotting flesh, the sea of emaciated people begging for food, the flies as thick as storm clouds, shallow graves filled with inky corpses. Here, there were no killings, but people died in droves from disease, starvation and exposure. And yet the human spirit rose above such deprivation. At Katma there were makeshift church services; deported priests tried to bury the dead with dignity and a small market was established.

'She met my mother? I can hardly believe it.'

'She met a pregnant woman with green eyes by the name of Arakelian, wife of a doctor from Caesaria.'

'In what circumstances did she meet my mother?'

'This woman was a refugee from Hadjin. She and her family camped beside your mother. They soon realised Gadarine Arakelian was no ordinary peasant woman.'

'What do you mean?'

'Your mother spent her time tending to the sick. When she wasn't nursing others, she went from tent to tent with a picture of her children, asking if anyone had seen them.'

I knew the photograph Farid was referring to but I was not convinced he was telling the truth. Many

Armenians had been duped by agents like Farid, hopes raised only to be dashed.

'What else can you tell me?

'There's one more thing and it's not good news, I'm afraid.'

'What is it?'

'Your sister was very sick and is unlikely to have survived.'

My heart sank. His story had frayed. 'I saw my sister die, Farid. What on earth are you talking about?'

'The woman said the doctor's wife travelled with a daughter by the name of Alitz.'

A lump clogged my throat. Farid was telling the truth. I had never thought to tell him about Alitz Tavlian when he had asked for information about my mother. She was the girl who travelled with us when her mother was snatched.

'Anything else, Farid? Anything at all?'

'Yes, the woman heard that your mother managed to bribe her way out of Katma. She boarded a train with Alitz, headed for Aleppo. I made inquiries through friends in the city but nothing more came to light.'

Aleppo. The funnel through which thousands of Armenian exiles were filtered on their way to relocation centres, as the Ottomans called them, in the barren deserts of Syria and Mesopotamia.

'Was there anyone travelling with my mother?'

'I couldn't trace any of the people you listed. I'm sorry.'

'What now, Farid? Where do we go from here?'

'There's nothing more I can do for you, I'm afraid.'

Leaving Farid, slivers of hope pierced my heart. My mother had been sighted, she had boarded a train with Alitz, survived hunger, disease and exhaustion. She was alive and I would find her and the child she carried and we would all be a family again.

Walking south along Victoria Street, I was a boy again, pacing the streets of Caesaria. This part of the city, inhabited mostly by Turks and Armenians, was reminiscent of home. There were simple mud brick houses beside intricately designed Gothic structures. The outlines of minarets and belfries werc dulled by the heat haze. The cry of the muezzin rang out, calling followers to prayer, and the five fingers of Mount Pentadactylon filled the distance, as conspicuous a landmark as the mountain that framed my childhood home.

As I approached the VIP enclosure that looked down on the parade ground, I had a premonition that something would happen, something life changing. This feeling sat heavily in my stomach as British soldiers began to assemble and people closed in around me. I watched the island's most prominent citizens arrive and take their seats. Top civil servants and British expatriates in double-breasted suits and trilby hats; their wives in flared, belted skirts and colourful dresses. There were Greek, Turkish and Armenian guests too, friends of the British governor. The chief justice and his wife, the deputy governor and the island's administrative secretary. I snapped them all and they enjoyed their moment in the limelight, posing conspicuously for the camera.

Spectators began lining the walls of the Venetian

fortifications, their excited voices filling the air. They were a motley gathering. Suited professionals with greased back hair stood beside hatted peasant farmers in pantaloons and embroidered waistcoats. Style-conscious city dwellers, in printed summer dresses, rubbed shoulders with shapeless women wrapped in shawls.

I bumped into Partogh, out for the day, and while he watched through jaded eyes, I continued to take pictures. A military band was playing and the island's governor set out along the parade ground on horseback, wearing a silk sash, war medals, complete with a sword and plumed hat.

'The British certainly have a knack for pageantry,' I said.

'The Governor looks like a puffed-up peacock, if you ask me.'

The major general and then the troops filed by, saluting the VIPs: the Royal Navy, the mounted squadron, the parachute regiment and the regulars, flaunting their regimental colours. Royal Air Force planes roared over-head, heightening my sense of foreboding.

'Well, there's a show of military power if ever I saw one. A warning to anyone with a mind to rebel.'

'No one's here to make trouble, Gabriel. Everyone's enjoying the sight of a peacock riding a horse.'

'Can't you see beyond the pomp, Partogh? Sense danger in the air? Can't you see the gun-toting guards surrounding the VIPs, sniffing the crowds, ready to quell the mere hint of insurrection? It wasn't so long ago that the Greeks burned down Government House.'

After the uprising, the British administration hammered any opposition, banning political parties, demonstrations and public gatherings, curbing the power of the clergy. I had grown to understand the Greek desire to self-govern but respected the British for building schools and hospitals, for creating an efficient civil service and recruiting English-speaking Armenians. We were favoured because we had no axe to grind and posed no threat to the administration.

'This is all rather extravagant, don't you think? The rest of us have to make do with a birthday cake, and that's if we're lucky,' Partogh said.

'We have much to thank the British for.'

'Long live the King so we can all live in servitude.'

'The British have built roads and planted trees on the island's barren hills.'

'And eradicated pesky locusts, blah di blah. I know all the arguments in favour of the British, Gabriel, but they are not as democratic as they like to make out. They continue to imprison political opponents without trial, to sentence young men to death by the noose. How long do you think the Greeks will stand for that? The sporadic violence will escalate. This island is a powder keg ready to ignite.'

'The British are a powerful force with a strong army. Noone will invade this island with the British here. Besides, haven't we suffered enough, Partogh? Is it wrong to want stability?'

'At the cost of freedom?'

A woman's scream suddenly gripped my spine. I watched the police head for a spot on the periphery of the crowd, quickly close in on a scene of chaos, people running this way and that, men hollering. Was this what I had sensed? Had violence erupted?

'What's that hullabaloo, Gabriel?'

'I don't know. Let's go and see.'

I squeezed through the throng, with half a mind on my family, heading blindly towards the unknown while logic urged me back. *Flight not fight, Gabriel.* My legs carried me into the clamour while hysterical cries catapulted me back to that morning in Caesaria's main square when I last saw my father; to that other day in the mountain village when I lost my uncle Nareg.

I arrived at the scene to find a boy in short trousers on the ground, his head clamped down by the knee of a soldier, several guns aimed at his head. I quickly took in the backdrop. An old bike on its side, a school satchel lying open, several homemade petrol bombs in glass jars scattered in the dirt. Disaster had been averted, for the crowd, for the governor, for the chief justice. The defiant boy faced prison, torture, possible execution.

I took a picture, instinctively, and headed away with Partogh. Down below on the parade ground, the troops filed by, unaware of the commotion. As the parade drew to a close with a forty-one gun salute, I snapped my last photograph of the governor, and through a wide-angle lens I saw a familiar face in the crowd, the face of a youth who made my heart skip a beat, a handsome face framed by sandy hair and serious eyes.

Partogh turned to me. 'Gabriel. You look like you've seen a ghost.'

I had.

'I have to go, Partogh. I have to go.'

I charged through the crowd, fearing the boy might vanish, become an illusion. I was drenched in sweat by the time I reached him. My mind had not played tricks on me. He was the living image of Minas, my friend who had jumped from the clock tower, a handsome, earnest looking lad. His quizzical eyes were as dark and generously lashed as those of my old friend.'Gabriel, is that you?'

I turned to the man standing beside the boy and realised this was Yeprem, Minas' younger brother. We embraced, blubbering like a couple of old women while the boy observed through thoughtful, focused eyes.

'Baba, what's wrong?' he asked.

We drew apart, sizing one another up. We had parted as children and now we were both in our thirties, our features hardened by our troubled past.

'Is this your son?' I asked.

'Yes. This is Aharon.'

'Your uncle Minas and I were very good friends,' I said.

'My father says I look just like him.'

'Aharon has my brother's looks and his brains,' Yeprem said. 'He's an A-grade student. Wants to be an architect.'

This news filled me with joy and pride. Minas was gone but his spirit had been resurrected in his nephew.

'And what are you both doing in Cyprus? Don't tell me you live here?'

'We came for a family wedding. We'll be returning to Lebanon tomorrow.'

'Then you must let me take you both for something to eat. There's a wonderful tavern not far from here.'

We walked together through the crowds, my arm linked through Yeprem's, Aharon walking beside us. At the tavern, I ordered raki and meze and we drank to our health and the memory of those we had lost. We talked about the past, about our time at the orphanage and the close friendship we had formed.

'Minas was such a shrewd boy,' Yeprem said. 'He didn't trust anyone at the orphanage, noone but you. He singled you out, Gabriel, chose you as a friend, showed you where his money was hidden. His savings helped me buy my first school books.'

'He would have liked that.'

'And then God sent me Aharon in his image.'

Aharon listened, rapt, asked thought-provoking questions revealing maturity beyond his years. He was a wonderful child and my affection for him was instant.

When Aharon and Yeprem left the island, we kept in touch by letter. Several years later, Aharon came to stay with us for the summer and proved the most delightful houseguest. We played backgammon and discussed politics and I encouraged his growing interest in architecture, mythology and ancient history. His visits continued even when he won a scholarship to study in England. He came every summer and we all looked forward to his visits but it soon became apparent that Tamar, my beautiful girl, was the magnet that drew him. The day they got married was the happiest of my life, a day documented in photographs, snapped from every angle, from atmospheric shots of Tamar and

Aharon standing at the altar, until the night, when we were all drunk on raki, dancing on table tops, reeling like dervishes.

★★★

A key turns in the front door lock and Anahit walks in. She greets Jennifer, kisses her grandmother and pretends I don't exist.

'Would you like some tea, darling?' Marta asks. 'Jennifer has just come to interview your grandfather.'

'No. I won't be staying, Grandma. I've only come to get some clothes.'

My little sparrow has flown the nest, moved in with a gaggle of crows.

'When you have time, Anahit, I'd love to talk to you,' Jennifer says. 'The views of your generation are essential to my study. I need to know how you feel about being Armenian, to find out how things are changing from one generation to the next.'

'Things aren't changing. Especially where marriage is concerned. Women are still expected to settle down with a nice Armenian boy and keep house.'

'What's wrong with marrying an Armenian?' I say.

'What's wrong with marrying a non-Armenian?'

'It's cultural genocide. The undoing of everything your ancestors suffered for, everything I suffered for.'

'Don't use such overblown language, Grandfather.'

Even when she's angry she looks like my sister, her green eyes flashing like backlit emeralds.

'You're not going to marry him.'

171

'Not even my father can tell me what to do. I'm a big girl, if you hadn't noticed.'

'I'll never give you my blessing.'

'Do we really have to air our dirty laundry in public?' Marta says.

'You're the one always quoting medical facts, Papik. Well here's one for you. Mother Nature favours hybridisation for strengthening the human genome. So let me go forth and hybridise, for crying out loud.'

'So we can all disappear into obscurity.'

'It doesn't have to be that way, Mr Arakelian,' Jennifer says. 'My husband taught me to speak Armenian and Anahit can do the same . . . '

'Who asked you?'

'Papik! Don't be so rude. Let me apologise on behalf of my grandfather,' Anahit says. 'Since I've never heard him admit he's wrong. Now, I really must leave before I say something I'll regret.'

'No!' Marta intervenes. 'Your grandfather and I will leave so Jennifer can speak to you. Gabriel, go outside and play with your snake.'

Chapter 30

In the back seat of Partogh's car, my heart hammers in my chest. We are 1,000 metres above sea level, winding through the Troodos mountain range. Partogh hurtles around a hairpin bend and my whole body tenses. He turns to me from the driver's seat with a grin.

'We'll be there soon, my friend. Don't worry.'

'Keep your eyes on the damn road, Partogh.' I steal a glance from the window at the mountainside, huge slabs of rock rising above us. 'And slow down, will you?'

From the front passenger seat, Hovsepian offers me a mint.

'Why did I ever agree to this?'

The question is rhetorical, a fact lost on Partogh. 'Because you're a greedy blighter like the rest of us and don't like spending your money.'

'Why spend money when you can take advantage of nature's harvest,' Hovsepian says. 'Troodos is a veritable fresh air market.'

'Well, I won't be risking my life again for a basket of wild fungi.'

I glance again from the window. It's a hell of a long

way down. I close my eyes and try to quell the churning in my stomach.

Hovsepian leads me along a path where the mushrooms are profuse, leaving Partogh to search for wild asparagus. We pick flat-topped field mushrooms and add them to a basket already teeming with morels, oyster mushrooms and funeral bells.

'Have you had any more thoughts about the snake?' Hovsepian asks.

'Oh yes. I've electrified the fence.'

'Electrocution? Isn't that going a bit too far, Gabriel?'

'I don't think so?'

'How many volts?'

'Twelve.'

'I'm relieved you're not planning to kill him.'

'Kill who?'

'Harry.'

'I was talking about the other snake, Therko.'

'Thank God for that. I thought you'd lost your mind, my friend.' Hovsepian bends down to pick a handful of small umbrella mushrooms on thin stalks. 'What have we here? Magic mushrooms. Feed your son-in-law a couple of these and watch him turn into a blithering idiot. Then Marta and Anahit will see his true colours and join the crusade.'

'What crusade?' Partogh asks, appearing from behind a tree, his brows wagging.

'Against the white genocide.'

White as opposed to bloody. Hovsepian refers to the evil of assimilation, the curse of intermarriage, the biggest threat to our traditions, our language, our nation.

'You're a dinosaur, Hovsepian. An old, defunct creature that will soon be extinct. Let the young do as they please. Why should they be tied down, become victims of our past?'

'Because we as a people nearly ceased to exist.'

'Why us, God? Woe betide us,' Partogh says in a whiny voice. 'Give it a rest, Hovsepian. The best thing the young can do, as a tribute to the past, is make the best of their lives, get a good education, move on.'

'And marry well,' I add, with a disdainful twist of my lips.

'I promise you, Gabriel, you wouldn't have been happy with any man Anahit introduced you to. Noone would have lived up to the perfect groom. Not unless he was a brain surgeon whose family came from the right region of the homeland, etcetera, etcetera. I suggest we drown our sorrows with raki and drink to your granddaughter's good health and happiness.' He reaches for a flask in his inside pocket and slumps down beside me, unscrewing the lid and taking a swig. 'I love it up here,' he says, passing me the flask.

'What's there to love apart from the mushrooms?' I take a good glug, handing the flask to Hovsepian. 'I lost my uncle not far from here.'

'Let go of the past, my friend. All that stored up resentment isn't good for the soul.'

'The past is not like water in a toilet bowl. It can't be flushed away. It's a septic tank growing more rancid by the day.' I pull up a clutch of magic sprouts growing beside the log and absent-mindedly put them in my pocket.

Back home, Marta rewards our efforts by frying our gatherings with eggs and garlic. I sit in the back yard with Partogh, feasting on a dish fit for the gods. When we have finished, Marta serves homemade paklava and Partogh takes her hand and kisses it.

'That was truly delicious.'

'You men did all the hard work.'

'But you turned our raw ingredients into something magical. You are a sorceress, Marta.' He kisses her hand again.

'Stop flirting with my wife, you old dog. Keep your greasy lips to yourself.'

'Not until she tells me her secret recipe.'

'There's no secret, Partogh. I used fresh eggs, good olive oil, plenty of garlic and the mushrooms you foraged. I found a few extra in Gabriel's trouser pocket and I used those too.'

The mushrooms in my pocket! The ones I pulled from the base of a log. Suddenly, I feel nauseous, realising my wife has unknowingly pumped us full of a hallucinogenic drug.

'Another glass of raki, Gabriel?' Partogh asks. 'Let's drink a toast to your wife's culinary skills.'

'I think I've had enough to drink.'

'Well, that's a first,' Marta says. 'Gabriel turning down raki. Are you sick, dear?'

It has grown dark. The hum of cicadas crescendos while the sound of traffic thins. I sit holding the string, attached to the twig that holds up the box that will catch me a snake. Partogh is yapping like a hyena and his merriment is infectious. I hear myself chortling and tittering in response to Partogh's terrible impersonations of old Jacob and the community president and even Hovsepian. He scrambles up and waves a white serviette in the air.

'Armenians of the world unite. Join the scraggy necks in their crusade against the white onslaught. We must defend our nation. Whatever the cost. We shall fight them on the beaches and in barbecue shacks, in the taverns and the discotheques. We shall never surrender to the *odars*.'

He curtseys, sits down and starts to hiccup. 'I feel very peculiar. This raki is strong stuff.'

I see a movement in the yard, near my box. I think it is real but it may well be a hallucination. 'What's that?'

'What's what?'

'Over there. I saw a movement by the trap.'

'Good Lord, Gabriel, I think it's the snake. Pull the string, man. Pull the string.'

I manage to dislodge the twig and capture the enemy.

'What do we do now, Gabriel?'

'Give the blighter a lift to the other end of town and let him feed off someone else.'

I grab the forked stick in the yard and make my way to the trap, Partogh following cautiously behind me, still hiccupping.

'I hate snakes. They give me the creeps.' He leans on my arm as we inch closer to the box.

'You lift up the box, Partogh, and I'll trap the snake's head with the fork.'

'I'm not going anywhere near that box.'

'OK. I'll do it.'

We are both on our knees. I gingerly lift up a corner of the box using the stick and peer underneath. 'I can't see anything. It's too dark.'

We draw closer and squint through the opening. Two beady eyes stare back. A sudden movement towards our faces has us toppling backwards, the shock curing Partogh's hiccups. Our quarry is not a snake but a rat. It scuttles away and victory slides from my grasp.

Partogh is flat on his back, chuckling. 'Don't worry, Gabriel. If the trap doesn't work, your electrified fence will soon stop that snake in its tracks.'

'This place is a rat hole.'

'A rat trap,' Partogh quips.

'I miss my home. I hate this dump. Doesn't it get to you, Partogh? Losing everything we worked for. Everything we built, brick by brick.'

'What good will it do letting it get to me?'

'It would make you human.'

Twenty-two years ago, I was a man of property. Bitter but not yet twisted. On a chilly December night in 1963, I was at home with Marta. Tamar had come to Cyprus for Christmas with two-year-old Anahit, leaving her husband back in England. Suddenly, a thunderous roar rocked the house, as if lightning and an earthquake had cracked the land simultaneously. The blast was followed by bursts of automatic gunfire, by shouts and screams, and then the lights crashed, casting the house into darkness. It was not exactly out of the blue, we had suffered years of unrest between Turks and Greeks. The previous decade, explosions and street murders had been a regular feature of life in the Turkish quarter.

When bombs exploded, people scattered like ducks spattered with lead shot, only to reappear in clusters when the smoke settled and the glass was swept up, the dead and injured lifted away. Between attacks, people went about their daily lives, buying bread, stocking up on cured meats, chatting to their neighbours, enjoying the sun and the background hum of cicadas in the evenings. Fear came in short, terrifying bursts and was quickly forgotten.

That day in December, flames and smoke rose in the distance. I left the house to see what was happening. Neighbours stared anxiously from their windows, too shaken to venture outside. I kept to the shadows, startled when I heard shouts in Turkish.

'Stop! Who goes there?' A machine gun was aimed at me, positioned in the mouth of a road leading off Victoria Street. I relived the terror I had felt in the clearing all those years ago, a cold fever drenching my body. The machine gun was manned by Turkish Cypriot soldiers, one of whom stepped forward, ordering me to raise my hands to my head.

'What's your name?'

'Gabriel Arakelian. I'm Armenian.'

'Where do you live?'

'Victoria Street.'

'Why are you out?'

'I heard gunfire.'

'And thought you'd get yourself shot. Go home and stay inside.'

I hurried home on quivering legs, barricaded the door with heavy furniture, clamped the windows and wooden shutters and tried to block out the gun battle filtering through the walls. The Turkish militia had moved into our suburb. This was no longer a fight among civilians and irregulars but a turning point. We spent the night in pitch darkness, huddled on the living room floor. I held Marta's hand while our daughter and grandchild slept between us.

'I won't let them take our home,' I whispered. 'I won't lose everything again.'

'It won't come to that, Gabriel. This will all blow over in a couple of days.'

'I hope you're right, Marta. I hope to God you're right.'

Marta fell asleep but I stayed awake all night as I had in the wilderness when Mariam lay beside me. I had promised myself I would protect my sister and ultimately failed but I would not fail again. I watched my family sleep with the handle of a carving knife held in my hand. I was their lion, their giant grizzly. Every explosive crack made me start, kept me alert, the handle gripped so tightly my nails pierced the ball of my hand. That night, there was only one certainty in my life. I

180

would have killed any man who tried to harm my girls.

As darkness thinned, my thoughts turned to the island's recent history. The British no longer ruled, Cyprus had won its independence three years earlier and had acquired its own constitution. Peace, since then, had been shaky and had now come to an abrupt end. Tensions had been building for some time between the Greeks and Turks over political power and proposed amendments to the constitution. The Greek Cypriots wanted an end to the separatist Turkish Cypriot municipal councils, permitted by the British in 1958. Turkey would have invaded if it had not been for the Americans. Pockets of violence, vengeful acts of murder, arson and kidnap had escalated into a full-blown battle between Turkish militias and Greek Cypriot paramilitaries, between guerrillas on both sides of the ethnic divide.

By morning, the battle waned and birdsong announced daybreak. A military vehicle rumbled to a stop outside the house and there was a heavy thud at the door. A British soldier called out, insisting we evacuate the premises immediately. We had little choice but to follow a broad-shouldered sergeant to a truck parked a short distance away. Several neighbours were already seated in the back and greeted us with solemn faces. The street was filled with soldiers, hammering on doors, ushering people out of their homes. I helped my wife and daughter onto the truck and then took a step back, refusing to leave.

'What the hell are you doing?' Tamar cried, Anahit cradled in her arms.

'I'm staying with the house.'

'Are you trying to get yourself killed?'

'I'm staying.'

'Have you gone mad?'

'No. I have never felt saner.'

'Then, I'm staying too,' Marta said.

Tamar gripped her arm. 'You're not going anywhere.'

I closed my ears to their pleas, to Marta's tears. My family was safe and would survive without me, whatever happened. I would not be chased out of my home, run like a coward. I remembered the boy of nine who had been forced to flee and I refused to relive that episode of my life.

I turned away and headed back to the house. I couldn't bear to watch my family leave as I had once watched my mother and Alitz disappear into the unknown. Back inside the living room, I replaced the heavy furniture, turned on the radio and lay on the sofa, listening to updates on the status quo, falling asleep intermittently, waking to blasts of gunfire. And so it went on, day after day, for a fortnight. I consumed all the perishable foods, the bread, milk, cheese, all the fruit and vegetables, moving on to pulses, boiling up chickpeas, lentils and black-eyed beans, eating with no regard for taste, resorting to coffee to curb my hunger. I had enough food in the pantry to last two more weeks and appreciated Marta's tendency to keep the shelves well stocked.

I trawled through family albums, through all the stages of my daughter's life, pored over Marta's face from quiet, youthful beauty to sweet-faced older woman, growing more beautiful by the year, a dream of a wife, the ideal mother. I was a fortunate man and was sure my wife would be looked after by Tamar if anything should happen to me. I cried fat tears that dribbled down my chin and splashed the cellophane-coated pages.

Beyond the door, the fighting had intensified and spread across the island. Turkish jets flew over Nicosia and the army had established permanent posts, commanding strategic routes into the capital. British troops were positioned along the barbed wire blockades constructed around the Turkish sector of the city. I listened to news reports with a growing sense of dread and increasingly the house I had grown to love felt like a prison, the empty shell of a creature with its heart ripped out. Without Marta I felt abject loneliness and when my solitude became unbearable, I unhooked the pictures from our walls: my girl growing up, her wedding, cherished snaps of my grandchild, the sole surviving photograph of my father. I packed every last picture into a suitcase along with the negatives. This time, my memories, at the very least, would be saved. I waited for a break in the fighting, moved the furniture aside, stepped into daylight and walked, brandishing a white handkerchief, suitcase in my other hand, as I made my way to the nearby checkpoint at Ledra Palace.

The soldiers there directed me to the Armenian secondary school that had become a camp for refugees and housed my family. My son-in-law had arrived from England to lend a hand. He and Tamar had set up a makeshift school for the children in one room and Marta was in the kitchen, with the other women, preparing wheaty *harissa* in a large vat. She wept with relief when she saw me but was quick to wipe her tears.

Lunchtime was approaching and there were many mouths to feed.

In the days that followed, theories and predictions abounded, cautious, extreme and hopeful. Most believed they would return to their homes within a matter of days, weeks, months, certainly not years. This wasn't 1915. We hadn't been permanently expelled from our homeland but from a small suburb, only a short walk away, across a barbed wire partition. The evacuees waited in earnest for the ceasefire to be announced, for the soldiers to retreat back to their bases.

A week after I left the house, I was offered the opportunity to return, under UN escort, to gather a few belongings. I was driven through streets that had become a ragged base camp for the Turkish militia, found myself frozen at the threshold of a house no longer mine, a dirty, looted wreck. Marta's treasured glass animals, collected over twenty years, lay shattered on the floor: swans decapitated, cats smashed to pieces, dolphin shards spread across the floor. Dirty boots had trampled her cherished rugs and cupboard doors hung off their hinges. Many had trespassed: soldiers, guerrillas and civilians. I imagined them rooting through my possessions, filling their pockets, wantonly trashing. The bed had been stripped of sheets. Someone had taken an axe to the bedroom suite and curtains had been pulled down. I felt sick, angry, cheated, a small child again in a plundered townhouse.

The fighting in Nicosia ended when British forces intervened at the request of the president but our hopes of a return to the Turkish quarter were short lived.

Nicosia was separated into Greek and Turkish sectors, the entire Armenian community was expelled from the enclave and I became a refugee for the second time in my life. We lost our church, our community centre, our primary school and the company of close Turkish friends, like Begum, who were an intrinsic part of our daily lives.

'A penny for your thoughts,' Partogh says, spread out on the ground like a starfish.

'How can a man lose two homes in one lifetime through no fault of his own? When will we ever find peace, Partogh?'

'Not in this life, my friend.'

'I thought we had reached a turning point the day the flag of the republic was hoisted.'

'I thought so too.'

'I even cheered the arrival of the troops. My Turkish neighbour, Begum, made a banner saying: Freedom and peace-bringing soldiers, we welcome you to Cyprus.'

The first official day of independence: August 16th, 1960. Greek and Turkish soldiers arrived in Cyprus to join a tripartite force, to serve as a single unit with the aim of protecting the sovereignty of the island. Ten thousand Turkish Cypriots lined the city wall to welcome the first contingent of Turkish soldiers to land on the island in 82 years. The Greek army received the same tumultuous welcome, walking on myrtle-strewn streets to the sound of the Greek national anthem.

'What have we done to deserve such an appalling fate when so many others are blessed with comfortable homes and enough land for their children to build on and relatives they can't stand the sight of? What I would give for a strip of land, for a brother or a sister, for an interfering mother.'

'Our lives are in the hands of the gods, Gabriel.'

'We are pawns at their disposal.'

'Such is the fate of man. Think of our families and the trials they suffered.'

'There isn't a day I don't think about them and how their lives were wasted.'

'They live on, Gabriel, through a pair of hopeless vagabonds drunk on raki, through my son's smile and your daughter's eyes. Their legacy is as immortal as the stars. And there's a sight you don't see every day. Look up, Gabriel.'

'I can hardly look down. I'm flat on my back, man.'

'That's the constellation Ursa Minor, more commonly known as the Plough, a group of seven stars. Its twinkling eyes looked down on the ancients and will still be gleaming when we are dead and buried and turned to dust.'

'The seven stars are the souls of doomed lovers reunited in heaven.'

'I never knew you were such a romantic at heart.'

'My sister loved that story and it's one of my favourites. It gives me hope that one day we'll meet again, in heaven.'

'You think you're going to heaven!'

'I expect my sister to be there waiting with a bag of halva.'

'And some raki if you're lucky.'

A distant explosion has me grabbing Partogh's hand.

'Old friend, I didn't know you cared.'

'What was that, Partogh?'

'Only an exhaust pipe. Nothing to worry about.'

I close my eyes against the churning sky and give myself up to a foam cloud that lifts me higher and higher, and carries me to the stars and my sister.

Chapter 31

A fog of exhaust fumes cloaks me as I walk along the potholed road that leads home. A battered truck trundles past spewing thick smoke that throttles my lungs and makes me splutter, as if my life isn't enough of a wreck already. Earlier, I went to the Armenian club, hoping to drown my angst in a game of backgammon, some steaming black coffee and an argument with Partogh, but there was no one there except old Joseph the club caretaker, snoring and ungainly in the corner. I sat down for a while wondering where my so-called friends had disappeared to. Had the club moved to new premises? Was I being ostracized for offending someone or other? Was there a funeral? Whatever the reason I had cause to be annoyed. Angry with myself for allowing a significant detail to escape me. Angry with that chump Partogh for failing to inform me.

My day has been thrown off kilter and as I put my key in the lock and turn it I look forward to a calming glass of whisky filled to the brim. Not Marta's watered down stuff but the throat-burning, anger-melting Johnny Walker gold hidden in my closet. I push open the door to an almighty clamour.

'Surprise!'

The Armenian club has spewed its guts into my living room. Glasses of the amber nectar raised.

'You bastards. You nearly gave me a heart attack.'

'Don't worry,' Partogh says, grinning like a lunatic. 'Dr Mouradian is at hand in case your ticker packs up.'

'What in God's name are you all doing here drinking my whisky?'

'It's your birthday, Gabriel,' Marta says. 'We wanted to surprise you.'

I hate surprises, especially ones that cost me money but I keep schtum and allow my friends the rare liberty of embracing me, clanking their aged bones against mine. The table is spread with a feast fit for royalty, with lahmajoun, kofte ghemali, souberek, tabouleh, humous and chi kofte; the dishes wafting cumin, garlic, and lemon juice. I roll up a lahmajoun and take a bite, trying in vain to gulp away my concerns. My store cupboard has been emptied and my whisky guzzled by a dozen men with fuller pockets than mine.

Anahit walks through the open door. Her gaze is soft and forgiving and the lahmajoun clamps my throat. The moment reminds me of my wedding day, when the world receded as Marta tiptoed down the aisle. This vision is rudely interrupted by Harry who walks in behind her. Why did she bring him, today of all days? When she knew all my friends would be here? The club president is a nosy bastard and bound to ask what Harry does for a living and then word will spread that Gabriel Arakelian's educated granddaughter, a teacher at the English School, is marrying a Greek carpenter. Anahit correctly interprets my frown and shakes her head, taking Harry by the arm and leading him into the living room at which point old Joseph appears at the door, wiping sleep from his eyes.

'Why the hell didn't anyone wake me up?'

The Waters of Lake Bingeol plays on a small tape recorder balanced on the windowsill. I am happily drunk and surrounded by friends, the haunting Komitas melody ferrying me back to the landscape of my childhood, to summers spent in my grandmother's village where Mariam and I were free to roam and climb trees and paddle the brook. I ride the slipstream over a landscape rich with orchards of apple, pear and apricot, over red-tiled rooftops and an undulating countryside.

'Where have you disappeared to, Gabriel, my friend?' Hovsepian asks.

'I was back in the homeland.'

'And where is that exactly? I've spent so many years over here I sometimes forget.'

'Who can forget their *dzenentavayr*, the birth place where we took our first breath and hoped to take our last?'

'The place of no return. I often travel back in waking dreams,' Hovsepian says, and the men sitting round him agree with a slow shake of their heads. Where would I go if I had the chance to return? I'd visit my father's grave, stroll through the streets where I played as a boy with Mariam, visit the church of St Gregory where I sang in the choir beside my brother, stand outside my old house, if it still exists, letting memory envelop me.

Partogh walks into the backyard with Harry and Anahit. 'I thought it would be nice if Harry joined us,' he says. 'So we can all get to know him a little better.'

Harry and Anahit sit on the periphery of the group and chat with Doctor Mouradian. Old Jacob glances at Harry and taps me on the leg.

'Hey, Gabriel, who's that?' he asks.

'My granddaughter's friend.'

'Her fiancé,' Partogh says, slumping beside me, the meddling ass volunteering more information than is absolutely necessary.

'A Greek?'

'A fine, virile young man who will give Gabriel the great-grandson he has always wanted.' Partogh prods me with his bony elbow. 'Isn't that what you always harp on about, adding another heir to your retinue? A boy to hold your hand and listen to your stories and take the name of your father.'

'Not at any cost, Partogh.'

Anahit tunes into our conversation and turns to me with a Medusa glare.

'He's a marvellous boy, Gabriel,' Partogh says. 'I've just been chatting to him in the kitchen about the superiority of walnut over pine. He's a very articulate and passionate young man who certainly knows his wood.'

'So does a woodpecker.' I grab a handful of nuts and gnash away, washing them down with a gulp of whisky, wishing Partogh would zip it.

'What does the boy do?' old Jacob asks, threatening to expose my closely-guarded secret. I must think quickly, deflect attention from Jacob's inquiry. I grab my throat and cough, put on a convincing performance of a man choking on an unshelled walnut. Doctor Mouradian is up on his feet in an instant, pulling me out of my chair and performing a series of unseemly abdominal thrusts. Emergency averted, I breathe rhythmically while the doctor fingers my pulse. From the corner of my eye, I see Anahit somewhat aloof, not in the least worried about my health though Harry's eyes are feigning concern.

The next thing I know old Jacob is up on his feet pointing to the metal fence. 'Gabriel, there's a snake in your garden. A dirty great snake. By God, man, it might be poisonous.'

Harry quickly rises to his feet and strides towards the fence, his hand outstretched. I let him touch the fence, see him shiver and then fall flat on his back, his head smacking the concrete, as a jolt of electricity passes through him. Anahit cries out and rushes to his side with doctor Mouradian.

'Don't touch the fence, it's electrified,' I say.

'It's a bit late now,' Anahit shouts.

'How many volts, Gabriel? How many volts?' the doctor asks.

'Only twelve.'

Harry stirs, looks around in confusion.

'Harry! Are you allright, my love?' Anahit is frantic.

'It's OK, Anahit. I'm fine, darling. No need to worry yourself.' He reaches up to finger a lock of her hair, forgetting himself.

'My God, I thought you were dead!' she says, her

192

eyes flooding, her love for him evident to all, even the old dinosaur who is suddenly pricked by guilt. I reach for my whisky and slope off to the kitchen.

Harry and Anahit soon make an exit but the feasting continues well into the night. When the last guest has left, I head for my bedroom on tremulous legs ready to collapse. A key suddenly rattles in the front door and Anahit storms in and backs me against the wall.

'What the hell were you trying to do, Papik?'

'What are you talking about?'

Marta rushes out of the kitchen. 'What's going on?'

'Your husband tried to electrocute my fiancé.'

'Twelve volts wouldn't kill a mouse.'

'That was an accident, wasn't it?' Marta says.

'It was no accident.' Anahit says.

'We had guests, Gabriel. You should have been more careful.'

'Guests I knew nothing about. A party I never asked for.'

'Do you think old Jacob would have survived a bolt of electricity thrumming though his chest?' Anahit says.

'I'm sure your grandfather didn't mean for Harry to get hurt. That would be . . . well . . . downright cruel and malicious . . . and what's more . . . illegal. Look me in the eye, Gabriel, and tell me it was an accident.'

I have lied to Marta so many times but this untruth clings to my throat, won't budge however much I swallow.

'I don't believe it! You silly old man! You've crossed

the line this time, Gabriel. You've been nothing but a bully and I won't let you get away with it.'

The next day my requests are met with silent non-compliance, my questions remain unanswered. Two can play at that game, I tell myself, and I will be the better player. At first my punishment is a blessing because no one nags me about my whisky consumption, no one asks me to change my vest or socks. I play them at their own game, enjoying the benefits of being ostracised. I have the edge when it comes to stubbornness and play my part with consummate skill.

Several days pass and my enthusiasm for the game wanes. Inevitably, I am worn down, beaten into submission. *Please, talk to me, Marta,* I say, when my request for coffee is ignored. *This is ridiculous and childish,* I complain, making my own cack-handed lunch of bread and cheese, dining alone. A week later, I feel so lonely I could weep and do so, on several occasions, in the privacy of my bedroom. Slumped in my chair, I accept defeat, feeling utterly demoralised. I am nothing without family, nothing but a bag of bones and vital organs. *I'm sorry Marta,* I say weakly, when I can take no more. *Apologise to Anahit,* she says, *and mean it.* I apologise to my granddaughter feeling like a wicked schoolboy, knowing I will soon be forced to look my nemesis in the eye.

A fragile peace has been restored. The women chat in the kitchen: Marta, Anahit and Jennifer. In the living room, I fade out their chatter, flick through the pages of the Armenian paper, legs hoisted on a leather pouffe. Disaster stories grab my attention, tales of tragedy, earthquakes, forest fires and traffic accidents that confirm my belief that life is one giant ordeal from beginning to end and can turn on its head in an instant.

I skim-read a piece about the opening of a new Armenian care home in Fresno, California, that includes brief biographies about a number of residents. One woman in her seventies describes how she was expelled from her village in Eastern Turkey and became an orphan when her mother was abducted by an Arab horseman. She joined a caravan of exiles travelling south before making her way to New York and later Fresno. I have heard such anecdotes a thousand times over and I am just about to turn the page when the name Alitz Gregorian, formerly Tavlian, jumps out. My addled brain takes several seconds to place the name.

'Marta, Marta!' I call out, my heart racing.

She hurries into the room, ready for an argument. 'No. I won't pour you another glass of whisky, so don't ask.'

'I don't want whisky. I've just read something in the paper and I don't know what to make of it.'

'What is it?' Marta draws close.

'I've come across a name I recognise. A woman with the same name as the girl who travelled with my mother. Alitz Tavlian. She lives in a care home in Fresno.'

'Good Lord, Gabriel. Could it be the same person?'

'I don't know. What do I do, Marta? What do I do?'

'Anahit, come quickly. We need help.'

Anahit and Jennifer hurry into the room, scan the article while Marta explains its significance.

'Let me make some calls, Papik,' Anahit says, heading for the telephone.

I sit in a stupor, holding Marta's hand while Anahit calls the international operator and then the nursing home. Her conversation is short and to the point and when she puts down the receiver, she is smiling.

'I spoke to the nurse who looks after Alitz. Apparently, Alitz often talks about your mother. I asked if you could speak to her on the telephone but the nurse said she was hard of hearing. She suggested you might like to visit.'

I don't know what to think, how to feel. The discovery is so sudden and unexpected.

'We have to fly to Fresno, right away,' Marta says.

'Yes, but how? We don't have two pennies to rub together.'

'We'll ask the community for a loan.'

'I won't go to anyone cap in hand.'

'You can stay at my place. I'll give you the keys. I don't live far from Fresno,' Jennifer says. 'You won't have to worry about accommodation.'

'I'll call Mum. Tell her to book the flights,' Anahit says.

'I will not ask my daughter for money. I will sort this out myself.'

A rush of adrenalin carries me along the road towards the local precinct. I enter the watch repairer's and find the owner sitting at his workbench, staring at the innards of a small clock, a magnifying glass lodged in his left eye. I unhook my pocket watch.

'I want to sell this. How much will you give me?'

He views it through the eyeglass. 'It's not in very good condition.'

'It's an antique.'

'It's old and dented.'

'You'd be dented too if you were a hundred years old.'

'I'll give you fifty pounds.'

'It's solid silver and worth twenty times that amount. I paid a grand for that watch.'

'It's a replica, made in China.'

'Give it here, you crook, you thieving piece of dirt.' I snatch back the watch and walk home in a blind rage, straying several times into the path of oncoming traffic, igniting the wrath of drivers who swear from open windows. I have worked my whole life and have nothing to show for it. No nest egg I can draw on, no asset I can sell to pay for a ticket that will help me find out what happened to my mother.

Marta is waiting for me in the living room. She pushes me into a chair, her face animated.

'Sit down, Gabriel. Jennifer has something she wants to say.'

'Mr Arakelian. I'm leaving at the end of the week and I have wanted to say thank you for helping me with the study.'

I drum my foot, looking around for household items to sell.

'Your participation has been invaluable and your stories have made a deep impression on me.'

The solid silver picture frame on the mantle will have to be pawned.

'I would love you and Mrs Arakelian to come and visit me in California, to stay at my home.'

My wedding ring will have to go.

'I would like you to accept a gift and I won't take no for an answer. I'd like to pay for your tickets to America.'

I'll sell my camera.

'Gabriel! Did you hear what Jennifer just said? About the tickets.'

I am suddenly aware of the goings-on around me, surmise I am being offered charity. 'I won't let you do that, young lady. There is absolutely no way.'

'My husband has already booked the tickets, Mr Arakelian. We leave tomorrow.'

Chapter 32

Katerina

I start packing my suitcase, relieved to be leaving the island, an ocean stretch away from Ara. I have a fleeting vision of our day in the orchard and suffer a pang of intense longing when the phone rings and Jenny answers it, rolling her eyes as she holds out the receiver.

'It's him. He's down at reception. Wants to talk.'

Flushing, I shake my head, refusing to take the phone. Jenny obliges, as only a close friend would. She's polite but brisk, and slams down the receiver with a finality that is fitting but hardly helps to ease the knots in my chest. I scan the room for stray pieces of clothing, tidying them away hastily. Moments later there's a knock at the door and Jenny heads for the bathroom, refusing to collude. I try to relax, smooth my temple with my hands and summon a casual demeanour verging on the indifferent as I hover at the door, edging it open. Ara's tired eyes meet mine. 'Can I come in, Katerina?'

He follows me into the room. I'm too stirred to speak as I realise just how much I've missed his physical presence.

'How are you?' he asks. He scans my face, as I try to swallow the stone in my throat and recoup my voice.

'Glad to be going home ... back to family and

199

friends.' The words seem to imply he belongs in neither category.

'I have news, Katerina,' he says. 'My mother made some calls and heard about a man with the surname Arakelian. He lives in Nicosia. He may be related to your grandmother. I've got his address. I think we should go and find him.'

The suggestion strikes me as ridiculous, the trip a waste of time. 'I'm afraid it's not possible. I'm leaving this afternoon.'

He scans the bed, scattered with my belongings, as if sizing up the job at hand. 'Finish packing. We'll take your case with us. We can get to Nicosia and be back in time. I'll drop you off at the airport.'

Ara has borrowed his father's car and, climbing in, I angle my knees towards the passenger door, wishing I hadn't agreed to this pointless trip. The silence is thick with festering emotion and it's clear we have nothing left to say to each other. We wind out of Larnaca and join a motorway choked with midday traffic. I lean my head back and close my eyes, a monosyllabic exchange punctuating the journey till we reach the capital.

'This is Ledra Street,' Ara says, as we drive into the city, along a wide, congested road lined with an array of designer boutiques, smart cafés and bars bustling with people dressed to impress. The scene is bathed in sunlight and I yearn to stop, take a stroll, sip a cappuccino and soak in the buzzing street – but not with Ara. It's a frenetic mishmash of a place but it works:

ultramodern, glass-fronted edifices sprawl alongside century-old buildings erected by the British.

Ara turns off the main thoroughfare and drives through a maze of residential streets where a range of architectural styles co-habit: white-washed houses, colonial villas, greying apartment blocks. The traffic thins as we head away from the high street and into the heart of Nicosia's suburban hinterland. We drive past several precincts where patisseries, bakeries and kebab shops spread their aromatic wares through open doors, past a photographer's and a shabby watch repair shop, and finally pull up outside a magnolia, stuccoed bungalow with a lemon tree in the front garden and jasmine trailing the door.

'This is it, the address my mother gave me,' Ara says, detaching his seatbelt.

Ara taps several times on the front door, then peers through the front window into a room obscured by a net curtain.

'Doesn't look like there's anyone in. Let's try the neighbours.'

Next door's bell is answered by a bald man in a white vest, dotted with grease stains. He swallows a mouthful of food, wipes his lips on the back of his hand and a conversation sparks up in Greek, the man's features signifying displeasure. His voice is loud and somewhat aggressive in a way that I assume is simply a sign of Greek vivacity, until he shuts the door in Ara's face.

'Oh dear,' Ara says. 'Mr Arakelian isn't very popular with the neighbours.'

'What did he say?'

'That he's a miserable old goat who's always telling him to turn his music down.'

'And where is he?'

'In America. He left yesterday and won't be back for a week.'

'That's it, then. I won't get to meet him.'

'I can talk to him if you like, let you know what he says.'

Ara stands a breath away, his body warmth seeping into mine, a flustering, overwhelming sensation that makes me want to draw closer but I move away to show I won't be toyed with, and head back to the car.

'I need to get to the airport. I don't want to miss my plane.'

'Let's pass by my place first. My mother wants to say goodbye, if that's alright with you.'

At Ara's house, I plan a brief farewell to a generous woman who has offered the most memorable hospitality. Arpi greets me with a kiss on both cheeks and a tray of freshly baked pastries, golden crescent puffs with a minty halloumi filling. I sip coffee and munch the warm cheesy turnovers while Ara recounts our fruitless visit, before glancing at his watch and stirring to his feet.

'You can't leave now, Katerina,' Arpi says. 'This man may be a relative.'

'My flight's already booked.'

'I have a niece who works at the airport. We can change your flight.'

'My boss is expecting me back at work in two days.'

'Don't you have such a thing as compassionate leave in England? This is a family emergency, after all. Didn't you promise your mother you would find out as much as possible? It's only another week.'

Arpi's a very persuasive woman, but the idea still strikes me as absurd. 'I've just checked out of the hotel. Where would I stay?' Besides, I'm out of money.

'You can stay here, in Ara's old room.'

'I can't possibly do that, Arpi.'

'Why not? I want you to. We both do, don't we, son?'

There's little enthusiasm in his nod, his face set, expressionless, while I'm at a loss, dazed by spiralling events.

'Why don't you let your mother decide?' she says. 'Give her a ring. Please.'

I call Mum and tell her about the man in Nicosia, the Arakelian that might be a relative.

'Katerina, this is wonderful news. You've come so far –you simply have to stay,' she says. 'Perhaps I should book a flight and come over myself.'

'This could all lead to nothing, Mum. Wait until I've checked him out before you start celebrating. Besides, what's so significant about finding out you're distantly related to some stranger who lives 2,000 miles away?'

'It's important to me and it should be that way for you too. Your grandmother was the only link we had to a culture we know so little about. If there's any chance this man's related to us, we need to know. He could be linked to that remarkable woman in the half picture who went through so much.'

'Does it mean that much to you?'

'Right now, it means everything to me and, one day, it's going to mean a whole lot more to you.'

I don't admit that in recent weeks, I've been staring at my face in the mirror until I don't know quite who I am, Katerina, Mariam, her mother. I've started to wonder which side of the family *my* children will resemble, what traits they'll inherit. I've been jotting down, ready to share, all the hand-me-down stories about our ancestors who lived on another continent, who were caught up in a terrible chapter of history.

In the kitchen, Arpi is eager to hear my answer.

'Mum wants me to stay but I should find myself a hotel.'

'I won't hear of it. Now, where's your case?'

'In the car.'

Ara carries my case to the room, then leaves me at the door while Arpi fusses, bringing towels and an extra blanket. The room is free of childhood paraphernalia, the walls freshly painted white, the bedcover pink patchwork. Nothing alludes to Ara's musical tastes, boyhood hobbies and preoccupations. The only point of real interest is a framed photograph on the bedside table and, left alone, I pick it up. A willowy old man with a curved moustache holds the hand of a small, curly haired boy, the pair standing beneath a citrus tree, orange globes of fruit shining out of the dull picture. I own a similar photo, girl in pigtails holding Gran's hand in her backyard orchard and the memory brings pangs of longing. While many girls model themselves on their mothers I wanted to be just like Gran – elegant and original.

Chapter 33

Gabriel

The Ativan I swallowed on the flight has done little to calm my nerves. I am fretful and apprehensive, hurrying ahead of Marta and Anahit, along the paved driveway that leads to a large, red-brick building, overlooking a well-tended front garden with a grassy lawn, trimmed hedges and neat flowerbeds. A ramp with handrails on either side leads to a double door entrance arched by the words: *Fresno Armenian Home.*

Inside, a sombre-looking man sits behind a desk, fiddling with his neatly trimmed beard as we sign in and mark down the time of our arrival. The reception area is clean and office-like with several doors leading off it. Far off sounds drift into the hallway. The low hum of a television set. Dice clattering against wood. The tremulous soprano voice of some old dear singing an operetta to piano accompaniment. The aroma of meat juices and root vegetables tinges the air, mingling with the mothball smell of old age.

The bearded man warmly introduces himself, insisting we call him Daniel. Then he promptly leads the way up a flight of stairs to a clinical corridor with a linoleum floor and sturdy handrails attached to the walls. Halfway along, he pokes his head through a partially open door.

'Mrs Gregorian, your guests have arrived.' He turns to me. 'Please wait here. I need to remind Mrs Gregorian who you are and why you're here. She can remember the past in minute detail but the present tends to elude her.'

I'm suddenly perspiring, petrified of hearing the truth. 'You go in, Marta. I'll wait outside. Just tell me what she says.'

Marta grips me by the hand. 'We haven't come all this way so you can skulk out here. You've waited a lifetime for news about your mother.'

Daniel reappears. 'She's ready for you now. Please, go in.'

He moves aside and we enter a large, colourful room, an antidote to the sterile corridor. The partially drawn curtains are blue silk. Shelves are lined with an array of books and magazines. An embroidered bedspread in a bold Armenian pattern covers a double divan. Vibrant paintings of Mount Ararat with its snow-tipped peaks decorate the walls. There are family photographs on every ledge and tabletop: a black and white wedding photograph; pictures of curly haired children; several young people adorned with mortar boards.

Alitz sits hunched in a velvet armchair, staring into her lap, a crocheted shawl wrapped around her shoulders, her silver-grey hair pulled back in a bun. A lacy blanket covers her legs and hands, leaving only her small, slippered feet exposed. Daniel introduces us all before directing me to a chair opposite Alitz. Marta and Anahit hover at the back of the room, their faces hopeful, expectant. Alitz looks up, peering through milky blue eyes, her face thin and bony, her skin translucent and dotted with liver spots. Age has not been kind.

'Hello Gabriel,' she says. 'I believe we met briefly before you were taken away.'

She slides a thin, veiny hand from under the blanket and hands me a photo, black and white, scored with jagged lines, a picture of three children in their Sunday best. I see Tovmas for the first time in over seventy years, his face the image of my father's. I see Mariam, the person I have missed most of all, the bright girl with such promise. I turn to my granddaughter. 'You see, Anahit. I told you my sister was a beauty, just like you.'

My wife and daughter stand over my shoulder, looking at the siblings they have come to know in stories, like characters in a fairy tale.

'Can you tell us what happened to Gabriel's mother?' Marta asks.

'Oh yes. I can. Gadarine took me under her wing. Treated me like a daughter. I will never forget her.'

The mention of my mother's name brings tears to my eyes. A flood of emotion, tightly contained over the years, hovers on the brink.

'What happened after you left Katma?' I dare to ask.

'How did you know we reached Katma?'

'Many years ago I hired an agent to find my mother. He traced her to the transit camp.'

'After Katma, we were conveyed to the desert of Der Zor. It was a terrible place. Blisteringly hot. We were both sick and weak. By then, your mother had lost the will to live. She was convinced the baby inside her was dead and she had given up hope of finding her children alive. She used to say, *I paid to have my children slaughtered.* We lay side by side in that desert waiting for death to take us. I kept hallucinating, images of my mother and father flashing in my mind. One minute I was at home with my family and the next I was in a scorching wasteland, my skin blistered and broken. And then, out of the blue, something miraculous happened.

'A Bedouin Arab took pity on us. He took us to a camp a short distance away, where small children played around a cluster of tents. In one of those tents, shielded from the glare of the sun, we both fell asleep on straw mats, while a young woman with dark, plaited hair gave us fluids to rehydrate our bodies. She nursed us back to health with those drinks and with meat cooked in a fire pit, with bread and fruit and hot tea. It was in that tent that your mother gave birth. The Bedouin woman delivered the child. We all shed tears when that baby boy took his first breath.'

'Gadarine saw her son, held him briefly in her arms and named him Grigor, after your father, and then, I'm afraid, your mother bled to death. A haemorrhage ended your mother's life, not starvation.'

Silent tears stream down my cheeks, along the groove made by the blade of a bayonet. I think of the years I have spent searching for my mother, always believing I could feel her life force.

'The Bedouin dug a hole in the ground for Gadarine, a metre from his tent, and carefully lowered her into it. The woman stepped forward and began to pray, chanting *el mulleh ra-ha-meen,* God is full of mercy, and then others from the tribe gathered round and many had tears in their eyes. I hope you can take some comfort from the fact that your mother was buried with dignity in the desert of Der Zor.'

I am frozen in time, hardly believing where I am and what I am hearing. I keep my lips firm, fearing the sounds I might utter, struggling with all my strength to acknowledge the truth, at last.

'Several weeks later, when the Bedouins were ready to move on, the man who saved me rode me back to the refugee camp and left me there. I travelled with a family to Damascus and later we managed to sail to New York where an Armenian couple adopted me. They were truly wonderful people. They treated mc very well. I am a very lucky woman, Gabriel. I lost my family but I grew up feeling loved and then I met my dear husband, Sargis Gregorian, and moved to Fresno. There's my Sargis in that picture.' She points to a wedding photo on her coffee table and starts to chatter about her husband. My thoughts snag. A vital detail has been skipped over and I struggle to remember what it is.

'What happened to the baby, Mrs Gregorian?' Marta asks.

This is the question that hangs in the air and offers a ray of hope.

'The baby passed away not long after Gadarine. The Bedouin woman wrapped him in her shawl and buried him with his mother.'

Alitz leans back in her chair and a desert landscape fills my head, visions of my baby brother being lowered into a grave of sand. There is no other life force beckoning, no Arakelian out in the world waiting to be found. All these years I had hoped in vain. I sit numbly, on the edge of grief, wishing with all my heart that I had never come.

We take a cab to the Armenian church in Fresno, a short ride from the nursing home. The road is tree-lined, shabby, populated by buildings under construction. Marta's and Anahit's chatter washes over me. I feel like a man who has suffered a brain injury.

The interior of the church is of lustrous sandstone; stained light plays on the sinewy body of Christ suspended above the pulpit. On any other day, I might have stopped to reflect, to chat about the architectural merits of the building, discuss its symbolism, pore over the icons. Today, it takes all my concentration to place one foot in front of the other and stop myself from collapsing. Today, the smell of incense and candle wax is an irritation.

We light candles for Gadarine and my infant brother, and mumble prayers, before sitting at the back of the church on a wooden pew.

'How are you feeling?' Marta asks.

'All my life I have felt a life force reaching out to me. I believed the child, at least, had survived, that one day we would meet face to face. '

'Isn't it better to know the truth than live a lie?'

'No, Marta. It's better to have hope.'

The sound of a choir filters in from an adjacent room, angelic voices, taking me back to the church of St Gregory, the day of Esther's wedding. My vision blurs while the pictures inside my head grow brilliantly vivid.

Pictures of Esther's wedding race through my mind like a deck of cards being shuffled. I see my childhood friend in a white dress, a coil of red hair escaping her veil. I see people from the past, hear an ancient liturgy in my ears, an auditory illusion.

I drift back to the dry plain where I last saw my mother, to the clearing where I left Mariam and Tovmas. Emotion chokes me and old sorrows rekindle one after the other. I see myself from above, the lens pulling back: a grey-haired old man inside a church, a pinhead in a vast country, miles from home. I am a boy again, in a boat, sailing away from my mother, cast adrift in a vast sea. A belt tightens around my chest and I struggle to breathe, choke on smoky air, my eyes streaming, a heavy weight pressing against my rib cage. I hear Marta's voice from afar. *Gabriel, are you all right? Gabriel, slow your breathing.* Anahit takes me by the shoulders and lies me on the bench. I draw long, deep breaths until the panic subsides and I am soaked in perspiration, head spinning in a grey haze, Marta kneels beside me, stroking my hair with her healing fingers.

'You'll be alright, Gabriel. You'll be fine, my love.'

'I want to go home, Marta. I want to go home.'

Chapter 34

Marta stands outside my bedroom waiting for Doctor Mouradian's verdict. I have been in bed for a week, staring up at the ceiling, refusing to eat, taking only occasional sips of water. I have held onto hope as a life source and now, deprived, I am nothing but a wisp of stale air.

Jennifer managed to rearrange our tickets. Two days after we arrived in Fresno, we boarded a plane and returned to Cyprus. The moment we stepped foot in the house, I took to my bed, the news about my mother and the baby too great a burden. My will to live has gone but my hearing is as good as it ever was and I focus involuntarily on the conversation outside my door.

'I don't know what to say to you. I wish I could do more to help,' the doctor says.

'What do you mean?'

'Short of dragging him out of bed, I don't see what I can do. He says he doesn't want to go on living.'

'You can't just decide to die, can you? Only God decides such things.'

'He's suffering from severe depression.'

'He'll get better, won't he?'

'If he doesn't eat or drink, his body will quickly break

down and then we could have real problems. If he gets too dehydrated, we may have to take him into hospital and feed him intravenously.'

'Surely, it won't come to that.'

'I can't rule it out. I've known people to give up on life after some traumatic event, usually after losing a spouse. Intense grief can affect the body adversely, increase heart rate, blood pressure, spasms, etcetera, etcetera.'

'I've been avoiding the call to Tamar, hoping he would come to his senses but she'll never forgive me if anything happens to him and I kept her in the dark.'

'Call her, Marta. You and Anahit shouldn't have to suffer this alone.'

'What can I do?'

'Make him feel life's worth living. Support him as much as you can. I'll call a friend of mine who might be able to help. A doctor from Limassol, a specialist. She's dealt with several cases like this.'

Later, I wake up to find Marta sitting beside my bed, Partogh pacing the room. Marta offers me water through a straw. I refuse in spite of my thirst and tears fill her eyes.

'Aren't you sick of lying down?' Partogh says.

I don't reply.

He opens the wardrobe and takes out my bottle of hidden whisky. 'Then I'll just have to drink this precious stuff on my own.'

He unscrews the lid, takes a noisy glug, smacking his lips together theatrically. 'That's good stuff, Gabriel. I'll take it home with me, if you don't mind. You won't be needing it where you're going.'

He takes a packet of Rothmans from his shirt pocket and lights a cigarette though he hasn't smoked in twenty years.

'Haven't you missed the evil weed? Won't you share a cigarette with your old chum? A dying man's last indulgence.' He stands over the bed, glaring and puffing voluminously. 'I've a good mind to find that snake and put it in your bloody bed, let the blighter bite you where it hurts. That'll get you up. Think what you're doing to your wife, your granddaughter. You're putting them through hell, you ridiculous old man.'

Marta lays a hand on his arm. 'Don't upset yourself, Partogh. Go home. Leave him to me.'

Partogh leaves with an exasperated huff and my wife strokes my hair. I show no sign of the tingling pleasure I feel, a river of tears brimming in my eyes. I imagine her touching me this way when I'm gone, when she dresses me for the coffin. I have to find a way to make her stop before emotion betrays me.

'I don't want to see Partogh again,' I say.

'Because he drank your whisky?'

'I don't want to see him or anyone else.'

'Why are you doing this to us, Gabriel? Why are you making us suffer?'

I turn away and cover my face with the sheet.

Harry is next to visit, standing sheepishly at the end of the bed with Anahit, a tight smile on his face.

'How are you feeling, Mr Arakelian?' A strange question to ask a dying man. 'My parents send their best.'

I doubt it.

Anahit comes close, laying a package beside me on the bed, wrapped in brown paper. 'Harry never got a chance to give you your birthday present. We thought you might like to see it. I'll open it for you, shall I?'

She tears off the paper revealing a walnut box with a gold lock. 'Harry made it. Isn't it lovely?'

The piece is accomplished, the work of a craftsman, reminiscent of the wooden spice box Mariam once owned, her memory making my throat swell.

'You love it, don't you? I knew you would. Get up now, please. Stop all this nonsense, grandfather.'

This isn't a seminal moment when sorrows are cast aside, when the invalid rises from his wheelchair and totters upright and we all fall in love and dance to the sound of violins. Real life isn't like that. It's rank and messy. Loose ends don't magically tie up with the granting of a gift.

'Talk to us, grandfather. Please.'

'Go away. I want to be alone, and don't bring *him* here again.'

Harry charges out of the room followed by Anahit and an argument erupts outside the door.

'He didn't mean it, Harry. He's a sick man.'

'Sick in the head.'

'Harry!'

'Well, it's true and you know it.'

'Perhaps, we should put the wedding on hold. Until he gets better.'

'It's not until next year. He'll come round to the idea by then.'

'He'll never come round to the idea of us.'

'What are you saying? That you're giving in after all this time? Can't you see this is a ploy to make you do what he wants?'

'He's suffering.'

'He knows how to play you, Anahit. He's getting exactly what he wants. He's a manipulative old bastard.'

'I didn't know you felt like that.'

'How do you want me to feel about a man who treats me like dirt?'

'He could die.'

'He won't die. That man will live forever to twist you round his little finger. You don't want to postpone the wedding. You want to cancel it, that's what you're saying.'

'I need to focus on my grandfather. You have to understand.'

'I've been more than understanding for long enough. Hiding myself away. Grinning like an ape in the face of your grandfather's rudeness. Allowing myself to be denigrated, bullied, even electrocuted.'

'He didn't mean for that to happen.'

'Stop lying to yourself. Why don't I make this easy for you? We're over, Anahit. Finished. Before you ask, I don't want to be your friend or wait another year to marry you. Find yourself an Armenian doctor and leave me alone.'

Harry's hurried footsteps recede and the sound of Anahit's tears cuts right through me and I wish for death to take me quickly and put my family out of their misery.

Chapter 35

Katerina

I grow accustomed to the pattern of life in Ara's house. Arpi stirs every morning to a chorus of birdsong, to sweep the veranda and prepare breakfast. Stray cats collect in the backyard to be fed before curling up on the garden furniture to sleep in patches of sunlight. Ara's father consumes a hearty breakfast before going to work and then Arpi and I have the place to ourselves. She makes coffee and slices sweet, spiced tea bread as we sit and chat, mostly about the neighbours, before we head out on a leisurely walk to buy ingredients. The fruit and vegetable mart, a short walk away, is stuffed with all kinds of produce I've never seen before: knobbly purple roots and lush, fan-shaped greens, spiky fruit, olives the size of gobstoppers and tomatoes as plump as grapefruit. I follow Arpi's lead, touching, sniffing and tasting, in a shop with no pre-packed wrapping in sight.

Back home, she makes a start on lunch. Sandwiches are anathema in Arpi's house. She fries and stews and bakes, concocts bulgur wheat salad with fresh herbs, uses a plethora of spices ground in a pestle and mortar, flavours desserts with orange blossom water she play-fully flicks in my hair. Her speciality is *kataifi*, a syrupy dessert that looks like shredded wheat, as well as rice

218

flour pudding that's pure comfort. I take to the pace of Arpi's routine with ease and while she cooks and chats and gives me small plates of food to sample, profound contentment settles over me, as if I've undergone life-changing therapy.

I'm not so relaxed, however, when Ara arrives home for lunch each day, because he still has a disconcerting power over me. Just a glance has my skin flushing but I hide it well and lunch is generally pleasant, if a little awkward. After we've eaten, Ara leaves while I return to his room and stretch out on his bed, rekindling my love affair with books. It's just what I need, a minor overhaul, ambrosia for the body and soul, time to ponder the contents of Gran's journal.

Every evening, the food fest resumes, usually outdoors, on the veranda, occasionally with friends. Arpi spills into overdrive, conjuring an array of meze consisting of olives, crumbly cheese, various salads and dips, spiced meat and the leftovers from lunch. We eat al fresco beneath a string of lights and sip wine till we're moderately tipsy, feeding feral cats titbits while Apollo prefers to stay inside, napping on his cushion in the front room. Armenian music plays in the background, a haunting melody sung to the accompaniment of a woodwind instrument, a *duduk*, Arpi tells me. Music that's risen through the ages strikes the deepest vein and transcends me to another world.

One lunchtime, Arpi comes into the spare room to find me gazing at the framed photograph on the bedside table.

'That's Ara and his grandfather,' she says. 'They had a very special bond. My father moved in with us when my mother died, God rest her soul. Ara took you to his orchard, didn't he?'

The memory brings a glow to my cheeks and I wonder what other details Ara has shared with his mother.

'They used to go up there at weekends, just the two of them, then return home with baskets of fruit and stories about their adventures in the mountains. My father was a jovial, life-affirming man, not one of these difficult old pensioners you hear about, and Ara loved him dearly. We lost him seventeen years ago and I remember that day as if it were yesterday. It was Ara's eleventh birthday and just after he'd blown out the candles on his cake, my father retired to his room. Several hours later, Ara went to rouse him and found he had passed away in his sleep. It was a terrible shock and took quite a toll on everyone, especially my son.'

Arpi looks me in the eye and I sense she wants to confide further but doesn't quite know how. She looks away, scans the walls and neatly ordered shelves.

'This room used to be stuffed to the rafters with all sorts of oddities he collected with his grandfather. You see, when Ara becomes attached, he can't bear to let go. He's like that with his sculptures and exactly the same way with people.'

I think of Nazeli and her childhood connection with Ara and his coldness suddenly makes sense.

The week passes quickly and, finally, the day arrives for Ara to drive me to Nicosia. We hardly speak in the car and I prefer it that way, no empty chitchat, no pretence at being friends though Arpi's veiled comments lurk at the back of my mind. I open a book and zone out, until we pull up, once again, outside the magnolia bungalow.

Ara knocks and I stand behind him, clutching Gran's journal. A woman in her late twenties half-opens the door and her face has me gaping. I'm staring in the mirror at an older twin, eyes the same shade of green, softly coiled hair just like mine. The hair could be a coincidence, in a land where spiral curls are the norm, but those eyes, a rarity, are beyond rational explanation. Ara turns to look at me, raising his brows. He's seen it too, the eerie similarity, but the woman seems too agitated to notice anything, cowering behind the door.

'Can we speak to Mr Arakelian,' Ara says. 'Is he in?'

'Yes. But he's too ill to speak to anyone.' She's from England, the North, if I had to hazard a guess.

'Are you related to him?'

'I'm his granddaughter.'

'Then perhaps we could speak to you?'

'I'm afraid it's not a good time. We're expecting the doctor at any moment.'

'Can we come back, when it's convenient?'

'Yes. In an hour. I really can't talk now.'

She closes the door with an apologetic smile and leaves us on the doorstep with time on our hands.

'Let's go for a walk,' Ara says. 'There's a place not far from here I think you'll like.' This is the most personal he's been for some time and a sliver of pleasure and recognition runs through my veins.

We set off in silence along the uneven road, into an area where the houses are turn-of-the-century, up an incline towards an old stone church, set atop a rocky outcrop. A bell tower and cupola are covered in weathered, red brick tiles and the windows are small and narrow, the building part church, part fortress.

Ara tells me this is the church of St Dhometios, built in the 1700s.

This is just how I envisage the church of St Gregory and for a moment I'm in Gran's young shoes climbing the paved steps that lead to the entrance. It's a hot day and the sun bounces off the ochre stone, toasts my bare shoulders. Standing in the shade of a eucalyptus tree, I look down over red-tiled rooftops and quaint houses with wooden shutters, my grandmother's childhood vista. Cicadas strum a calming refrain. A light breeze strums the leaves. I feel strangely at peace and childhood memories come flooding. Sleepovers at Gran's, warm biscuits waiting in the morning. Movie nights with popcorn and fizzy drinks, hour upon hour of girl talk in the kitchen. The care she took over cuts and scrapes, those lingering gazes that told me I was the most important person in her life, that she loved me unconditionally.

Gran's story wasn't all black. She had a happy childhood before her life began to unravel, a happiness that was as formative as the tragedy that followed. She was the victim of a terrible chain of events but she was also the product of a loving mother, a doting father and two splendid brothers; she had a second family that considered her a gift from God. They all left their mark, shaped her in distinct ways, made her the wonderful woman she was.

We buy warm halloumi buns from the local bakery and break off chunks as we walk. I don't feel any inclination to exert myself for Ara's sake. I remind myself that, after today, I'll never have dealings with him again. I see a watch shop up ahead and step inside while Ara, obligingly, waits on the street. The man at the counter has a magnifying glass in his eye, his bench littered with metal scraps layered in dust. I take my great-grandfather's pocket watch out of my bag and hand it to the man.

'Is there any chance of getting this fixed?'

He takes a close look at the watch and gives his head a slow shake. 'How strange. A local man tried to sell me a replica of this watch very recently. This is the real thing. Very valuable. You should take good care of it, my dear.'

'I just keep it in my bag.'

'I suggest you buy a case and get it insured.'

'Can you get it working?'

He opens up the back and does something dexterous with his fingers before rummaging through a drawer below the counter. He brings out a small key, pops it the back, winds it several times until the watch comes to life after so many years of lying silent. I buy a case before I leave, a black leather cover, with the last of my spending money.

An hour later, the woman invites us into the house. It's old-fashioned with a worn nest of sofas at one end and a large dining table at the other. The walls are hung with family photos in gilt-edged and wooden frames, pictures cramming every square inch of wall: smiling children, parents and children, grandchildren duplicated in various poses.

'Please, take a seat,' she says. 'How can I help you?'

'I'm Ara Kupelian.'

'You're Armenian?'

'Yes. And this is my friend, Katerina Knight, from England. Her great grandmother's name was Mariam Arakelian.'

Her eyes widen in surprise. 'That's my great-grandmother's name.'

'The family came from Caesaria.'

The woman smiles. 'So, there's a very good chance we're distantly related. Wait, let me call my grandmother, Marta.'

Anahit ushers in her grandmother, a petite woman with grey hair pinned back, and we are quickly introduced.

'Distant relatives do occasionally crop up,' Marta says, standing over her granddaughter's chair.

'My great-grandfather was apparently a doctor. His name was Grigor.'

Mother and granddaughter glance at each other. 'My great-grandfather was a doctor by the same name,' Anahit says. 'This is very odd. It can't be the same man. That would be impossible.'

'I have a picture of Gadarine in my bag.'

I take out the journal. Squeezed within its pages is the torn photograph. Anahit turns to her mother. 'This can't be happening.'

Marta hurries to the sideboard where a black and white picture of a man with slicked back hair takes pride of place. She removes the backing, extracts the photo and lays it on the coffee table. It's torn down one side and when I place my picture down, it becomes whole, the dismembered hand finally finding its arm.

'Where on earth did you get this picture?' Anahit's tone is incredulous.

'It belonged to my grandmother. It's a picture of her mother.'

'No! That's impossible,' Anahit says. 'My great-grandparents had three children. Gabriel, Mariam and . . .'

'Tovmas.'

'Yes.'

'Gabriel and Tovmas died.'

'No.' Anahit shakes her head. 'My grandfather, Gabriel, saw both of his siblings die in very tragic circumstances. He saw them die.'

'I think you should both sit down,' Ara says. 'Katerina, hand me your grandmother's journal.'

Marta and Anahit clasp each other's hands on the sofa while Ara reads from the journal taking us back to a clearing where children are gathered, expecting to be fed, where guards circle them like sharks. The women are well-acquainted with this story and it affects them instantly, their eyes filling. They listen to the story of the girl who was buried beneath a mound of bodies, who clawed the ground when danger had passed and crawled from the scene, covered in blood and gore, who buried her brother, Tovmas, and wandered away, full

225

of remorse for leaving Gabriel in the jumble of bodies. The women are immersed in a tearful embrace, before they turn their eyes on me.

'Gabriel survived, Katerina,' Marta says. 'He was saved by an exceptional Turkish woman who happened to be passing. He was a breath away from death but she nursed him back to health. If this is true, then my husband is your great uncle.'

Anahit's eyes meet mine, river green, her face a blend of Gran's and Mum's and mine, and while my head says this just can't be true, my heart and guts know otherwise. Somewhere in this house there's a man who's been dead for more than seventy years, a fictional hero come to life. My head spins while Ara shares everything we know about my grandmother, her upbringing and the couple who saved her. The two women debate how best to break the news to Gabriel.

'He's really unwell,' Marta says. 'This will be very emotional for him but we'll just have to tell him. Come on, Katerina. If this doesn't get him out of bed, nothing will.'

I hesitate for a moment, a niggling voice in the back of my mind saying *what if it isn't him?* How will I handle the disappointment? I want the man to be Gran's brother more than I've wanted anything in my life. Ara takes my hand and leads me along a dark hall, a queasy vertigo taking hold. In a stuffy bedroom an old, pale-faced man is lying on his back, staring up at the ceiling . . .

I sense the arrival of two strangers. They stand at the end of the bed staring like undertakers sizing me up

226

for a coffin. For some reason, Marta decides to rake up the past, sparking my irritation, reeling off my life as a nine-year-old boy, taking me back to that march in the wilderness, the day in the clearing when I lost my brother and sister.

'The story didn't end as you thought,' she says. 'Something miraculous happened, Gabriel dear. Your sister survived. Did you hear that, Gabriel? Your sister did not die.'

I flush with anger, my eyes imploring her to stop her nonsense.

'Mariam was saved by a nurse and went on to live a long and happy life. She died only recently but she had a daughter.'

I never imagined my wife could be so cruel. What is she trying to do? Shock me out of bed?

'This young lady is Mariam's granddaughter, Gabriel.'

I shift onto my elbows, summoning the little strength I have left. 'Is this some kind of sick joke?'

'No, it's not. Katerina, come close.'

A young woman approaches, a fusion of my sister and my mother, dark waves trailing her back, and just for I moment I think I've woken up in heaven.

'Why are you doing this to me, Marta?'

'I'm not doing anything to you. Show him the picture, Katerina.'

The young woman hands me a black and white photograph of my mother, the woman I have idolised all my life, the picture I handed to Mariam the day we were ousted from our home.

'How did you get this? What the hell do you want from me?' I raise my voice and the girl steps back with a start.

'You'll regret you ever spoke in that way,' Marta says. 'Katerina, tell him about your grandmother.'

'My grandmother came from a place called Caesaria. Her parents were Gadarine and Grigor. She was separated from her mother when her family was forced to flee the city. She lived her whole life thinking both her brothers were dead.'

My hands quiver, my head boils, anger refusing to subside. 'What was the name of her older brother?'

'Tovmas. He had brown eyes flecked with gold. He was in love with a girl called Esther and dreamed of reaching America.'

'Why are you doing this to me, young lady?'

'This is Mariam's granddaughter, Gabriel. Do you understand?'

She has my sister's eyes but still I refuse to believe.

'My grandmother named my mother after you. She used to talk about your love of sweets and the fun you had together . . . '

I wish the girl would stop, but she goes on and on and my chest grows heavy, jabs at my ribcage. It's not what she says that affects me so much, as the way she says it, her expressions reminding me so much of Mariam, the smile in her eyes, the way her pretty nose wrinkles. I recognise the symptoms of a panic attack even as I experience them, even as I think I'm about to die. I gasp for breath, choke on turbulent air, that ghastly belt tightening around my chest again.

228

'Call the doctor. Quickly, call Doctor Mouradian,' Marta cries and Anahit hurries out of the room.

The girl lays something cold and heavy in my palm, closes my fingers around it. I find myself wishing to see what it is but my blasted arm won't move, the object pulsing like a heart inside my hand. The girl draws my hand close to my face and I unfurl my fingers and see the back of a pocket watch like my father's but still I don't believe until my eyes focus on the inscription: *Grigor Arakelian*. My visitor smiles, Mariam's beautiful smile, and then I realise that I had not hoped in vain, that the day I had dreamed of all my life has finally materialised.

She lays her head on my chest, soft curls falling across my face, scented with orange blossom. I stroke her hair with clumsy old hands and my heart relaxes for the first time in eons and the tears flow, leaching every ancient misery out of me, great sobs that make my body convulse and take away my breath. I weep for all the beloved people I have lost, but most of all I shed tears of divine happiness for the angel whose cheek lies against my heartbeat.

Anahit dashes back into the room. 'The doctor's on his way.'

'I don't need a doctor. I need my clothes, a box of tissues and a stiff drink, if Partogh has left any of my whisky.'

Marta is beaming and the lovely girl lifts her head to look at me with those unmistakable green eyes that set my sister apart.

Marta and Anahit head for the kitchen to make tea while Katerina rings her mother, and hands me the

229

receiver. Through another round of sobs, I hear my niece's voice, gather my breath to tell her I can't wait to see her and hold her in my arms.

In the evening, we all sit down and eat and drink wine with a ravenous hunger, and I sing drunkenly. All too soon, it is time for Katerina to leave, but she promises to return early the next day, to stay for as long as she can. I am too excited to sleep. I want to go on talking and drinking, sharing this immeasurable joy with my family. I go in search of Anahit and find her in the hallway, speaking to Harry on the telephone, recounting the events of the evening. I am happy but for the stone in my shoe, the sadness I have caused her.

I wait for her to finish her call, then approach with an apologetic smile. 'Anahit. I have something to say. You know, I'm not good at apologies but . . . '

Anahit puts a finger to her lips. 'Don't speak. Don't say a word, grandfather. Just listen. The wedding will go ahead whether you like it or not. I love Harry with all my heart. He is my future and I won't give him up. Not for you. Not for anyone. And one more thing, that may or may not be of interest to you, I'm having a baby.'

Life hands me another gift, another blessing. I kiss my granddaughter, squeezing her, but not too tight. I make a point of calling my nemesis to congratulate him, call him *son*, blub like a baby, drenching the receiver with tears. I am a silly man and always will be, but I am not as silly as Hovsepian.

Chapter 36

Katerina

It's past midnight when we leave Great Uncle Gabriel's house, feeling light-footed, elated. We have spent the evening celebrating a resurrection, the reconnection of our fractured family. Brother and sister never had the chance to touch and share their lives, but, I would like to believe, they could sense each other's presence through the ether.

Ara hovered on the fringes of the gathering all night and I'm suddenly aware that he has been the instigator, the catalyst for such joy –for giving life to a dying man. I voice my gratitude and he reminds me that my family's story is part of his heritage too. There's no awkwardness between us on our slow drive back to Larnaca as we chatter incessantly, all animosity cast aside.

Arpi is waiting up for us, eager to hear all about it. When she finally goes to bed, I sit on the veranda with Ara, sipping the remnants of her soothing aniseed tea. We mull over Gran's childhood, the happy times with her family in Caesaria, the security and love she found with Rose and Ernest. I tilt my face to the heavens, to focus on a peppering of stars in a Mediterranean sky sparkling with celestial mystery. I don't count them. I want to believe there are seven, that Gran, her parents,

Rose, Ernest, Tovmas and Esther are gathered together above us, reunited.

We sit back, reaping the splendid silence until Ara speaks.

'I need to explain why I never turned up, why I didn't call.'

'There's no need. I know you still have feelings for Nazeli.'

He shakes his head vigorously. 'Not at all! Whatever gave you that idea? I never had strong feelings for Nazeli.'

I recall Arpi's words about her son's inability to let go, and wonder whether I misunderstood her message.

'I couldn't face you, Katerina. I said too much, made a fool of myself. You told me to live for the now but I couldn't do that –not with you.'

I recall how I felt when Rob dealt the same card, told me to savour the moment, every word a punch to the heart.

'I'm sorry.'

'Don't be. You want to get back to your world, your family and friends. I understand that.'

'My world just got a whole lot bigger. I guess I'll have to spend more time here, now.'

'To be with your uncle Gabriel?'

'And do a spot of fruit picking. If you still need help?'

His smile is slow and infectious, spreading to his eyes.

'Where's that journal? The end of your grandmother's story has been preying on my mind. Are you ready for the last chapter?'

Chapter 37

Mariam

It was Christmas Eve, 1921. I had just turned fifteen and my old life was becoming a distant memory. I still suffered flashes of that day in the clearing but had settled into life with Rose and Ernest, living slow-paced days defined by lessons, chores, after-dinner walks, cold nights by the fire,

Ernest's sister, Irene, arrived with her family at midday. She was a plump, gregarious woman with two teenage sons, Edward and Marcus. Her husband Jack played the harmonica. I always looked forward to their visits when the small house would come alive, the evenings spent playing card games and singing carols and popular tunes.

We hadn't seen them for a year and the boys had shot up. Edward's sandy hair had grown and he wore it swept back in a style that struck me as decadent. He was sixteen, the same age as Levon, wore a brown leather jacket that made him look older, an impression rein-forced by the cigarette he smoked in the garden later that day.

His welcome was a bear hug, an embrace so tight I could barely breathe. 'What's happened to you?' he said, finally releasing me, standing back to absorb the

233

whole. I felt self-conscious in my knitted pullover, a dark green turtleneck that I had outgrown.

'You're so beautiful, Mariam,' he said, squeezing me again. Over his shoulder, I saw Levon's eyes narrow.

After lunch, Rose and Irene headed for the kitchen to start preparations for Christmas dinner, stuffing a goose, making cranberry sauce, wrapping sausages in bacon, steaming a plum pudding. Levon joined them in the kitchen, stuffing cabbage leaves for our evening meal. He had taught himself to cook and three times a week Rose gave him free rein in the kitchen, turned a blind eye to the upheaval.

Ernest had surrendered a corner of the garden where Levon planted herbs and his interest in cooking had become obsessive. Rose produced the same stock dishes week after week, stews and boiled ham, roast dinners and sponge puddings. Levon experimented, spending his kitchen days in a frenzy, concocting inventive meals, a fusion of East and West, trying to replicate his mother's recipes. He liked to cook alone, to shout and vent his frustrations when his experiments failed to meet his expectations.

I played cards with the boys in Ernest's workshop where Edward lit a cigarette and blew smoke rings. He talked about a life in London filled with friends and weekend dances and food that came in packets and tins, evenings spent listening to the radio. The boys were charming and attentive and never made me feel like the poorer cousin. Levon joined us, his cheeks red from the heat of the stove, his clothes and hair infused with savoury aromas.

'I've never met a man hooked on cooking,' Edward said. 'I'd much rather spend the afternoon with a gorgeous girl.'

He winked at me and I couldn't repress a smile. I was no longer the twiggy waif Rose had found, but a girl with curves swelling beneath thick sweaters. The heads that turned to stare at me in church still caused discomfort but there were no looks of pity. Young men flashed eyes tinged with admiration and desire.

'Levon wants to open a restaurant one day.' I tried to smooth the waters, sensing Levon was out of sorts.

'You'll have to come to London,' Edward said. 'You can't open up around here unless you want to serve sheep.'

'I can't wait to leave this place.' This was Levon's mantra but the thought of uprooting unnerved me, leaving Rose and Ernest and the settled life that had healed my wounds.

'Any nice girls in these parts?' Edward asked, oblivious to Levon's sullen mood. 'I bet all the boys round here are beating a path to your door, Mariam. If you weren't my cousin, I'd be first in line to ask you out.'

'She's not your cousin, so watch your mouth.'

Levon's hostility brought a rush of heat to my face. He had no right to behave in that way, to play the overprotective brother and spoil our Christmas. I gave him a look that told him so and ignored him for the rest of the day.

The next morning I woke to the smell of a Christmas roast and a warm feeling in the pit of my stomach. I had spent the night in Levon's single bed, having given my room up to Irene and Jack while he slept on the sofa. I had fallen asleep to the scent of his skin and the perfumed oil he used to tame his hair. I resented his moods but I couldn't stay annoyed for long.

There was a knock at the door and Rose walked in, holding a dress box tied with ribbon. She beamed at me.

'I think you should open this in private. Away from all the boys.'

The card read: *To a wonderful daughter, a gift from God*, the words ringed by a heart. I pulled off the ribbon, lifted the lid and saw a swathe of emerald silk.

'I asked Irene to find you a dress in London. You know, I haven't a clue about girls' fashion. I do hope you like it, Mariam.'

It was the kind of dress I had only ever seen in magazines, with a drop waist and a scooped, knee-length hem. It reminded me of the clothes I had worn on feast days and I pranced, delighted, around the room as if the dress were my dance partner. Rose helped me dress and then combed my hair, gently coaxing out the tangles. When she had finished, she fetched a bottle from the bathroom and splashed a clear liquid into her palm, smoothing it over my hair. The aroma of citrus filled the room, an essence she had made from orange blossom to remind me of home, the smell evoking memories of another mother, dressing me with silken fingers, her hands spice-scented.

Irene gave me my first lipstick that felt as precious as gold bullion in my hand. She applied a cupid's bow to my upper lip and led me to the full sized mirror fixed on the wardrobe door. I stared at my reflection, seeing a person I hardly recognised, an elegant, modern young woman, the person I wanted to be every day of the week. Hugging the dress to my body, I rushed out of the bedroom and down the stairs, meeting Levon's open-mouthed stare. My cheeks flushed and they grew hotter still when Edward wolf-whistled and Levon's awe-struck gaze followed me across the room.

I kept the dress on all day and noted Levon's stolen glances. He was crabby and distant, still in a sulk from the day before. I ignored him, set the dinner table with Edward and sat between the boys, enjoying their attention and the delicious spread. Potatoes roasted in goose fat, the bird served with cranberry sauce, roasted chestnuts, creamed turnips, Irene's Brussels sprouts and sweet carrots finished with butter and a sprinkling of sugar. For pudding we had chocolate bonbons and plum pudding with custard and Rose's Christmas cake, made the week before with candied peel, glace cherries and brandy. The men emptied the brandy bottle and each of the children was allowed a small measure. It was my first taste of alcohol. The fiery liquid flowed down my throat and into my belly, where its warm glow heightened my awareness of Levon's dejected glances. He was sullen throughout dinner while I enjoyed the most pleasurable Christmas of my life.

After dinner, Jack played harmonica and Irene sang. Edward grabbed me by the hands and we danced, the dress swishing around my legs as I spun just like I had on the day of Esther's wedding. Edward twirled me round

237

and round while I was blissfully aware that Levon was watching, though I never once looked him in the eye.

I fell into bed still wearing the dress, my head spinning. The house was silent but for Jack's snore, rattling like a motorcycle engine. A candle flickered on the window-sill, the flame casting shadows across the room. There was no malevolence in the shapes that formed and dissolved. I was nodding off when I heard a faint knock. Levon tiptoed into the room holding a bundle, wrapped in brown paper.

'I made this for you,' he said.

I sat up, giving Levon a gracious smile. He walked across the room to fetch the candle and perched beside me.

As I tore off the paper, I was a girl again, opening my father's gift on the feast day of St Sargis. Levon had made me a wooden spice box, on its lid the painting of a man and woman, sipping wine on a brightly coloured rug. The woman wore a yellow sari, her breast exposed. As a child, I had found the scene enchanting, magical, now I saw passion, erotic love and I realised why Levon had saved his gift until we were alone. I had described the box to him so many times and he had ventured inside my mind, seen through my eyes, painted a scene that was almost identical.

'I haven't finished the compartments yet. I'll do that in the New Year, I promise, have them ready for your birthday, fill them with your favourites: black pepper, crushed chillies and cinnamon.' Candlelight ignited his eyes and in them I saw how much he wanted me to love it.

I wrapped my arms around his neck and, finally, he smiled, his equanimity restored. I moved the box to one side and lifted the blanket as I had done so many times when we were younger and he had come to my room at night, fearing the dark, an invitation for him to climb in. He blew out the candle and lay down but his body was stiff and when I covered him, he shifted away from me.

'What's wrong?'

'Edward needs to watch himself.'

He turned to face me. 'I don't like the way he looks at you.'

He had always been protective of me but this was something different. He was jealous and this knowledge pleased me.

I drew close, laying a hand on his chest, and felt the contours of his body. He laced his fingers through mine and a fire burned in my belly, more intense than brandy flames. I lay rigid, holding my breath, relieved the darkness was hiding my blush.

He moved his face closer to mine, the outline of his cheek traced by moonlight, his eyes glistening. He leaned in to plant a gentle kiss on my lips and my heart pounded in my throat, the taste of his mouth too brief. I drew closer, kissed him again, aware of his lips, his sigh and the hand he gently ran down my body, pressing the silk against my skin. I was the woman in the utopian landscape painted on the lid of the spice box.

'I love you, Mariam,' he whispered.

'I love you, too.' The words, unspoken for so long, slid out.

We lay pressed together, legs entwined, speaking with

our eyes and then he sighed and drew away. 'I'd better go, before they find me here.'

I watched him leave, desperately wanting him to stay, for the night to go on forever. Sliding under the blanket, I stared at the ceiling, playing the kiss over and over in my mind.

There were more stolen kisses in the weeks that followed, in the woods beyond the house, in bed when Rose and Ernest slept. We lay awake together until morning, planning our future, the restaurant Levon would open and the home we would build. Nothing felt more natural than kissing him and yet I knew it was wrong to love him in this way. We had lived together as brother and sister. To our parents, friends and relatives, even in the eyes of the law, we were siblings with the same surname. We were being raised in a Christian home where virtue was a guiding principle and our actions taboo. We knew all about sin and righteousness. This knowledge was overshadowed by our growing love.

Elsie Barrow arrived from America one Sunday morning in August. It was a beautiful day, breezy and sunny, and I was sitting in the kitchen with a ravenous appetite waiting for Rose's bread rolls to bake. A month of good weather chimed with my mood, with the light-hearted optimism that carried me through each day. Levon too was less prone to sulks, though he continued to plan his escape. He had just got up when Elsie knocked at the front door. He answered, and led her into the kitchen. Rose looked delighted to see the old friend she had worked alongside in the Mission school and the two women embraced. When Ernest joined them the kitchen filled with sounds of excited chatter.

'Why didn't you tell me you were coming?' Rose said.

'I wanted to surprise you all, especially Levon.' She turned to him. 'I have splendid news, my boy.'

I waited, holding my breath, sensing that Elsie's next utterance would somehow change the course of my life.

'We've located your mother and your uncle Boghos. They're alive and well and living in New York. They're waiting for you, Levon, and can't wait to see you.'

Levon's eyes widened, they moistened and then he cried out, taking me in his arms. *I told you they would find us*, he repeated. The room was suddenly spilling with screams of excitement, joyful tears, talk of a miracle but the quiet part of my brain feared that there would be no happy ending. Rose and Ernest wrapped their arms around us, kissing our heads. We were all aware that this gain would lead to loss, that this miracle would accelerate the break-up of our family.

'What happens now?' Ernest asked, moving away, his voice fixed, his smile hiding what his eyes could not.

'We leave for America,' Elsie said.

'Did you hear that, Mariam? We're sailing to America.'

Levon stood back, refusing to understand why I had fallen limp, why Rose was sniffling into a handkerchief.

'What's wrong with everyone? Rose, why are you crying?'

'Surely you understand that Mariam won't be joining you. Your mother doesn't have the means to support

241

her and even if she did, this is Mariam's home,' Elsie said. 'She can come and visit when you're settled.'

'We'll all come,' Ernest said. 'Rose, dry your eyes. We knew this might happen one day.'

Levon clutched my hand. 'I won't leave without Mariam. You don't understand.'

'You must join your family,' Elsie said. 'We're leaving in seven days.'

My stomach lurched as the facts sank in. I pulled my hand free and bolted from the house. My heart pounded as I raced across the scrubby land beyond the lawn and into the coppice. I ran through the pain that gathered, aware that Levon was behind, calling out my name, wanting to get as far from him as I could. The force of his will had made this happen while I had lost all hope of being found. As I glanced over my shoulder, my foot caught in the undergrowth and I fell heavily, biting hard on my lip. A moment later, Levon was beside me, down on his knees, turning me onto my back, breathless. He took off his shirt to dab the corner of my mouth. I was dazed, in pain, and the taste of blood in my mouth took me back to the clearing where my brothers had died and this memory caused the tears to surge.

'Please, Mariam. Get up,' he said. 'Let's go back to the house and talk to Rose.'

He tried to enfold me in his arms but I pulled away, suddenly lashing out.

'Why are *you* crying, Levon? You've got what you wanted.'

'I don't want to leave without you. Come with me, Mariam.'

'This is my home. Rose is my mother. You heard what Elsie said. If you really loved me, you'd stay.'

I knew I was being unfair but at that moment, I felt Levon was choosing his mother over me, that his words of love amounted to nothing.

'I have to go, Mariam. But I'll come back for you, I promise.'

We lay side by side, felt every nuance of the parting still to come, waves of pain and sorrow. A life without Levon would be no life at all but he had to go, this was his fate. I couldn't leave Rose, give up my home a second time, the place where I had found peace, security and family love.

Levon stroked my hair, kissing my wet cheeks, my forehead and then my mouth. With a trembling hand, I unbuttoned my blouse and he traced a finger along my collarbone, sweeping his hand over me, setting my body alight. I had never felt so free, so brazen and courageous, so removed from the world, so sure of what I wanted. His fingers searched my body, soft, gentle fingers with incandescent tips that made me tremble and sigh. I folded my legs around his waist, drew him closer, our bodies moving one against the other, instinctively. I wanted to keep a part of him with me forever and closed my ears to the whisper, *no Mariam, we mustn't.*

Later, we walked back to the house, resigned and disconsolate. Grief had already set in and I closed my ears to Levon's promises about a future I no longer believed in. We barely spoke during the days that followed –there was nothing left to say. At night, he came to my bed and

I lay awake in his arms, willing time to stop, wishing his mother had never been found. A week later, I watched him leave from my bedroom window, my eyes glued to the path that led away from the house, until Levon had faded from sight just like my mother.

Losing Levon, I was thrust into the story of The Seven Stars. I spent long stretches of the day in bed, numb and empty, angry with God for stealing everyone I had ever loved. Gabriel had been wrong when he said no one died of a broken heart. Losing Levon, I felt a vital part of me perish, like soft tissue deprived of blood.

He wrote to me soon after he arrived in America but his letters offered no relief. He wrote of the happy reunion with his mother and uncle, about the family's struggle to make ends meet and the Armenian neighbourhood where they all lived in a tiny flat. He had exchanged a silent backwater for a sea of vibrant sound, for streets that bustled with life. He relished being amongst people, jostling for space on the sidewalk, hearing raised voices in our mother tongue, finding a community of Armenians with a church at their hub. He connected with the people in the neighbourhood, many of whom were refugees just like us . *They have dark skin, jet black hair, brooding eyes, troubled faces and handlebar moustaches. They are rough and comical and proud-looking and remind me of the people we grew up with,* he wrote. He soon found work in an Armenian restaurant and wrote of his plans to save money so that he could open a place of his own, make his fortune. Levon had found his spiritual home and it was clear to me that he would never return to England, that the spice box would never be finished. At my lowest ebb, I wanted to burn it, along with his letters, to banish every trace of him and forget he had ever existed, but I didn't have the heart. The box carried associations beyond Levon, memories of my father's feast day gift and mother's aromatic kitchen. I buried it beneath winter jumpers so I wouldn't be reminded of Levon and the promise he had broken.

I withdrew into my own small world. Rose and Ernest could do nothing to console me. I began reading the medical books I had found in the attic, the dog-eared copies of Sajous' medical journal and the Red Cross first aid manuals. Reading was a welcome distraction that kept me from brooding. I memorised the symptoms and treatments of diseases, pored over diagrams and instructions on how to set broken bones, dress wounds and prepare an antiseptic poultice. I recalled the patients my father had treated for burns – the children who had tumbled into cylindrical ovens dug in the ground, the adults burned by live coals from the brazier while cooking or warming their legs. The world of the human body and its malfunctions was vast and all-consuming. I lost myself in its depths, followed its contortions, its riddles, delighting in its detail and complexity. This was my father's domain and, entering it, I felt closer to him. Sometimes, when I read, I imagined him standing over my shoulder with an approving smile and this image spurred me on.

A month before Christmas, I was standing at my window, wrapped in a shawl. The cold pinched my cheeks and froze my breath into icy plumes. The woody, ephemeral aroma of winter jogged memories of the

245

previous year, of Christmas with Levon, our first kiss. A sharp pain stabbed my belly, subsided and then jabbed again, making me double over. I ran a hot bath and crouched in the steaming water. I lay still until the bath had grown cold and spots of blood appeared. Nauseous and dizzy, I climbed out, calling for Rose. She came at once, helped me into bed and sent Ernest to fetch the doctor.

That evening, a young doctor I had never seen before walked into my bedroom. His name was John Longshore. He ushered Rose and Ernest from the room before he examined me. I knew what had caused the pain and nausea, even before the doctor told me. He broke the news to Rose and Ernest outside the door and I heard cries of anguish, Ernest consoling Rose, the doctor's cool-headed replies pacifying them both. When they entered the room, my mouth filled with the taste of vomit.

'Whose is the baby?' Ernest asked, his eyes to the ground. 'Is it Stewart's?'

It took a while for me to realise they meant the farmer's son. They had no idea, not a clue of the love that had flowered beneath their roof, between the boy and girl they thought of as siblings, whose closeness they had always encouraged.

'Speak to us, Mariam. Who's the father?'

I owed them the truth, so I mouthed Levon's name. Rose sank to her knees and sobbed. Ernest stooped to take her in his arms.

Rose didn't speak to me for weeks while Ernest tiptoed between us, looking hurt, but every night they prayed for my recovery, seated on the chair beside the bed where they took turns to watch over me as the doctor had instructed.

Rose's coldness didn't last –she wasn't made that way. There was never any talk of giving up the baby or sending me away to hide from our small community and no suggestion of contacting Levon either. He was just seventeen, thousands of miles away, unable to support a wife, and to the outside world he was my brother. I was too young to believe such hurdles could be crossed, that Levon and I could make a life together. In the back of my mind, a niggling voice spoke of sin and the stain of incest, of forbidden love. I thought of writing to Levon, telling him about the baby, but I feared he might grow to resent me for forcing him back to England, robbing him of the life he loved. And how would his family receive the news? Would his mother accept me?

I was prescribed bed rest and, as the months passed, the doctor's visits became more frequent. I looked forward to them like nothing else. We had no other visitors and had stopped going to church. Ernest made weekly trips to the village store but I was hidden away from our small farming community, shielded from the rumours, protected from a world that scorned young women in my predicament, forced them to seek back-street abortions or declared them insane.

When the time came, Doctor Longshore and Rose delivered the baby and there was nothing but joy in the faces that greeted my daughter. The doctor held her in his arms and heard her first breath. When I embraced her, love flooded my heart, love more intense than I had ever known. When I cuddled my baby girl, breathing in her warm vanilla breath, I no longer ached for Levon. She was the family I had lost, her smile reminding me of Gabriel. Irene and the boys resumed their visits and grew to love the baby that blessed all our lives with her good nature.

Every night, I lulled her to sleep with my brother's stories, the sluice gates of my memory bursting open, liberating tales about Brave Nazar, about The Sun Maiden Arev and the man-eating wolf. John continued to visit, slotting into the quiet routine of our lives, joining us for meals in the evening when we would chat about his work, advances in medicine, the world beyond our neighbourhood peaks.

It was during my talks with John that my dream took shape of becoming a nurse and following in Rose's footsteps. Nothing made more sense than saving life when I had witnessed so many people die. John and Rose encouraged my ambition, bought me books and helped me to apply for a place at nursing school. Slowly, as the letters from America waned, my focus became Gaby and my studies and, in John's eyes, I began to notice the same intense longing that I had once seen in Levon's.

Chapter 38

Katerina

Great Uncle Gabriel asked Jennifer to make enquiries and within a matter of days she discovered an elderly man called Levon Petrosian, well-known as it happens, the owner of New York's most popular Armenian diner, The Seven Stars. This is no coincidence, I tell myself, remembering the story Gabriel passed onto Mariam who shared it with Levon, the tale that captured his imagination. Levon was lost for more than sixty years and found within four days. A week later, Mum and I board a plane headed for the Big Apple.

We hire a taxi from the airport straight to Manhattan, Mum holding my hand while I take in the landscape of TV shows and the big screen. Frenetic street life. Wide roads clogged with yellow cabs. Those proverbial geysers spewing steam. Overhanging traffic lights that look like Lego fishing rods. Mammoth billboards, an overwhelming predominance of high-rise concrete, steel and glass, hemming us in, obscuring the sky, while an ocean of pedestrians manoeuvre their way along the street. We pull up outside a glass-fronted building with a sign in bright blue letters, the words decorated with a halo of seven stars.

It's twelve noon and the place is already bustling with tourists and groups of dark-eyed diners occupying cosy nooks. The colourful, eclectic decor comes as little surprise. The Seven Stars pays homage to the homeland that Levon spoke of with such fondness and nostalgia. Vibrant paintings of a rugged landscape hang on the walls and murals have been painted on every free space, even on the ceiling. A novice hand has etched sun maidens and fire spirits, sorcerers, princes and thieves, all the characters Mariam wove into the tales she told Levon when they were children.

We sit down at a window table, the centre piece a bag of complementary halva wrapped in cellophane. A waiter approaches, with olive skin and thick, dark hair. He hands us a menu and asks if we would like to order drinks.

'Gin and tonic,' Mum says, hoping for courage in a glass.

The waiter scribbles on the notepad. 'Anything else?'

'Mum. Isn't there something you want to ask?'

'I can't handle this, Katerina. I'm trembling.'

'Everything OK?' the waiter asks.

'We're looking for a man called Levon Petrosian. I believe he owns this place.'

The waiter raises his eyebrows. 'He's in the kitchen, striving for perfection as usual. I'll see if I can prise him away.'

The waiter leaves and Mum leans across the table. 'Let's go, Katerina. Mum never told me about any of this. Perhaps, she didn't want me to know.'

'That's crossed my mind too.'

'This man might not want anything to do with me and I really couldn't handle that. And what about his family? How are they going to feel about a daughter turning up, out of the blue?'

'We've come too far to stop now.'

'We've already had our happy ending. I have an uncle, one I thought was dead, and I had a wonderful father. I don't need another one.'

'Don't you think *he* has a right to know?'

A mural catches my eye on the back wall. A boy with unkempt hair and large ears holds the hand of a girl with long wavy hair. The pair's feet are pointed as they float upwards towards a constellation of stars. This restaurant not only pays homage to a lost homeland but also to a lost love.

A smartly dressed old man walks across to our table. He is stately with thinning grey hair and, in his smile, I instantly see my mother.

'How can I help?' he asks, his rolling American accent stippled with Armenian.

'I'm Gaby Knight and this is my daughter, Katerina.' I have never seen my mother look so flustered.

'Ah, you're English. I have many customers from England. What can I do for you, dear ladies? I do hope you're not going to ask me for ketchup!'

Mum turns to me for help but I have no idea where to start so I open my bag and take out the spice box Mum brought with her as proof. Levon's good-natured smile fades as I place it into his hands.

'Where did you get this?'

'It belonged to my grandmother.'

Levon sits down heavily, his eyes on the box. He opens it, breathes in its lingering wood spice scent. 'I made this box, I gave it to a friend.'

'My mother's name was Mariam Longshore.' Mum has finally found the strength to speak.

Levon brings a hand to his mouth, catching his breath. 'Mariam? My Mariam?'

'She recently passed away.'

Levon's dark eyes spill as he pulls at the handkerchief tucked in his shirt pocket. 'Mariam's dead?' He buries his head in his hands, hiding the emotion that makes his body quiver.

'Please don't upset yourself,' Mum says. 'We've something to tell you.'

He looks up, his face sunken.

'My mother got married several years after you left.'

'I know. She married a doctor and she had the life she deserved. I probably shouldn't tell you this but I was deeply in love with your mother, well before she met your father, of course. She was the love of my life and I had to leave her behind. I came to America intent on making my fortune and giving her everything but the months slipped into years. By the time I had achieved my dream, she was married and I was heartbroken. I never recovered, never tied the knot myself. I'm not the kind of man who loves twice in one lifetime.'

Mum grips my hand. 'Katerina . . . '

'When Rose sent me a picture of your mother's wedding, my heart shattered.'

'My mother didn't have any pictures of her wedding.'

'In the picture I received she was holding a beautiful

252

little girl with dark hair. I didn't know who she was. I assumed she was one of your father's relatives.'

Mum's grip tightens. 'I must have been there, Katerina. That's why I remember the dress.'

I hold Levon's gaze and will him to understand. 'My mother was born nine months after you left.'

'What is it you're telling me, young lady? I'm an old man with a slow brain.'

'Mr Petrosian,' Mum says. 'My mother kept a journal. We know how close you were, how much she loved you. I've come to tell you that she never forgot you, that I have reason to believe I am your daughter.'

In Levon's face disbelief gives way to joy and then his eyes are streaming, my mother's too. He looks at our faces and bursts into tears, takes Mum in his arms across the table, kissing and squeezing and it seems he might never let go. Then a trembling hand reaches for mine and he turns to me, examining my face as if poring over a detailed map.

'I don't understand,' he says, shaking his head. 'Why didn't she tell me?'

'She was fifteen. She knew how much you loved your life in America and she couldn't leave Rose.'

'I blame myself. I was too busy to write, too poor to travel to England, to stubborn to give up my dream. Please tell me she was happy.'

'She was very happy. My grandfather was a great man.'

'You look just like her,' he says. 'Same eyes, same sweet little nose but I'm afraid, poor girl, you have the generous, Petrosian ears.'

253

He squeezes my hand against his cheek, setting me off and we are all crying while customers stare, cutlery posed mid-air.

The waiter approaches. 'Is everything OK, Mr Petrosian?'

'It's more than OK. It's wonderful. A dream.' Levon wipes his eyes and pats the waiter on the arm. 'I want you to meet my daughter and my granddaughter. Aren't they the most beautiful sight you've ever seen?'

'When did that happen?' The waiter raises his eyebrows.

'It's a very long story, my boy, one that began in 1915 and has reached me full circle. Now, bring us something to eat. All this crying has made me very hungry.'

'What shall I bring?'

'Everything. These two look like they need filling up.'

The waiter walks away with a puzzled expression and Levon motions towards the mural of the boy and girl. 'That was my Mariam. Long hair running down her back, the tiniest waist. Deep down, I always feared she was too good for me, too clever and pretty. I opened my diner and called it The Seven Stars in the hope that if she ever came to New York and walked past, she would know exactly where to find me.

'Do you know how I made my fortune? By selling these.' He lifts the bag of halva in the cellophane wrapper. 'Made to the same recipe Mariam and I concocted one day in Rose's kitchen, with sugar and marshmallows and chocolates. Not exactly traditional, I know, but delicious nonetheless, and the Americans seem to like them. I used to tell them it was made from a secret, age-old Armenian

254

recipe handed down through the generations. I could hardly say it was the product of a boy with a sweet tooth who had to use whatever ingredients were at hand, a boy who wanted to impress the girl he adored.'

Levon is everything I imagined and hoped he would be. Gregarious and open-hearted, affectionate and charming. We talk non-stop about the journal, the years he missed, the reunion with Uncle Gabriel.

The food arrives, dishes I recognise and have grown to love. Spicy shish and soft flatbread, flavour-packed dips. Cold dishes dressed with oil and lemon. Salads laden with parsley and pomegranate. Vine leaves stuffed with rice and pine nuts. I feel a sense of belonging in Levon's decorative diner, before these plates of familiar food, a sense that Mum and I have embarked on a journey of discovery that will last a lifetime.

Levon runs his hand along the lid of the wooden box. 'So, she kept this with her all her life.'

He lifts the lid, revealing the unread letters, and pulls one out.

'We think these were written to you and never sent. We have no idea what they say.'

'Would you like me to tell you?'

He unfolds a letter, holds it close to his face and reads:

Dearest Gabriel,

I have found my own way to remember, to celebrate the past and resurrect fond memories, a ritual requiring pen and paper. I sit beneath my favourite oak and write to you in our mother tongue. When I think of you, the words spill out of me onto paper, purging me of all my

255

secret thoughts. The others have left me, one by one, even Levon, but your spirit travels with me, surfs my shadow, watches over me, your image preserved faithfully in the locked chambers of my memory. I read my letters to an audience of chestnut trees and oaks, to robins and passing squirrels.

Do you remember New Year in Caesaria when we were children, how we waited for gifts? One year you wanted a wooden horse and I had my heart set on a doll. Mama told us to write to St Nicholas with our wish list. On January 1st, we woke up to find the presents we had hoped for and believed our letters had worked their magic. I pen your letters with the same childlike hope that my sentiments will reach you in heaven, where I am sure your soul waits for mine.

I often imagine you as a grown man, if you had lived and I had died, if our fates had been reversed. I don't visualise a saintly brother, bathed in haloed light but a formidable character with an irrepressible wit, a storyteller with a sweet tooth, a loveable rogue with a piquant tongue. I wish you had been able to share my life, hold my daughter and look into the eyes of a girl who reminds me so much of you. I was very young when she was born but more than ready to be her mother.

One day, when I can find the words, I will tell her that she was created on the day I felt most alive, that I loved her father with all my heart and have never looked back with regret . . .

Levon breaks off, choked.

Mum sniffs through her handkerchief. 'She wanted

me to know but couldn't find the words to tell me. The only person she could share her thoughts with was Gabriel.'

The letters in the box are not addressed to an old love, as we had thought, but to a lost brother.

When we finish, Levon says he'd like to take us somewhere, a short cab ride from the diner. Out on the street, while we wait, my mind turns to Ara and the distance between us, a vast stretch of ocean and sky, an eleven-hour plane journey, a whole seven days. Our relationship is on hold while this chapter of my life plays out but the longing has returned, an intense desire I have never known before, coupled with rekindled thoughts about the future.

In the cab, Levon points out the spire of St Vartan's Cathedral, a modern rendition of an ancient church building, strangely at home in this busy section of Manhattan, populated by tower blocks and a maze of shops and restaurants. We cross a rectangular courtyard, climb a set of stone steps and enter the cathedral's wooden doors. The vast interior with its gentle lighting, scented with incense, feels unearthly, a sacred space in the heart of New York City. The musty silence is punctuated by the click of our footsteps on the stone floor and intermittent coughing. Several worshippers mill about or sit on the wooden pews in quiet contemplation, their heads lowered in prayer.

Arches span the edifice. Six narrow windows run from floor to ceiling and Gothic-style chandeliers hang overhead. We crane our necks to view the underside of

257

the dome, supported by a crown of four arches. Stained glass sheds a rainbow of light, illuminating the painted symbols that circle the cupola.

'This is where I come to escape the hustle and bustle,' Levon says. 'To remember Mariam.'

We all light candles for Gran and the gesture is strangely cathartic. I'm not a churchgoer but, standing in this sacred space, I feel moved, immersed in the divine and a sense of heritage unexplored.

Levon stands next to me. 'I never thought I'd have a granddaughter and one so delightful. I never thought I would hear anyone call me grandfather. What would you like to do on your first day in New York?'

'I hear they sell wonderful ice-cream here.'

'In a multitude of flavours.'

Mum is a girl again, happy at the thought of ice-cream.

I take Levon's arm. 'I like pistachio and strawberry cheesecake.'

'My favourites. You definitely have my genes.'

'Lead the way, Grandpa.'

'Katerina *jan*,' he says, calling me his dearest, turning to look at me with teary eyes. 'I don't suppose you could say that one more time.'

Chapter 39

Nicosia, Cyprus, 1986

I stand next to Ara outside the eighteenth century church on the hill, posing for a picture beside Harry and Anahit, a baby bump rising beneath the folds of her wedding dress. Guests surround us. Mum sandwiched between Dad and Levon, all with beaming smiles. Great Uncle Gabriel bends over a tripod, adjusts his camera and continues taking multiple shots.

A feast awaits at a nearby hotel. Tables have been set with every conceivable delicacy Marta and Levon could conjure, a feast fit for deities, for the sun and moon. Gran's treasure box resides in Gabriel's kitchen, finally finished with compartments gifted by Harry, filled to the rim with flaked, crushed and powdered spices in vibrant hues.

Gabriel snaps more pictures, asks the children to squat, demands smiles, his passion for photography rekindled along with his zest for life. He has long-term plans that require him to live: to visit England, teach Mum the language of her ancestors, see his great niece married off to a suitable Armenian boy, with a nudge and wink in Ara's direction.

Cyprus means much more to me now than it did on my first visit, an island where I have family and

259

newfound friends, a place I must visit again and again to carry out research for the book I'm writing, with the help of my translator, of course. A saga about an extraordinary family that will be passed down the genealogical line for generations to come.

'Let's all move to the brow of the hill,' Gabriel says, 'for one last shot.'

We assemble haphazardly.

'I'll set the timer for this one,' he says.

He fiddles with the dial and lightly sprints to stand beside me and, taking my arm, he dons the same look of pride he wore when he watched Anahit walk down the aisle. We stand before a stone bench, a piece of rough-hewn rock, bleached white by the sun, a charming, misshapen fusion of Gaudi and the Flintstones. An emblem that will be here, overlooking the city, long after we have all gone. A place for quiet contemplation. A bed for feral cats beneath the shade of a eucalyptus tree. A seat of stone inscribed with the words: *In memory of a wonderful mother, sister, caregiver and cook, who performed culinary alchemy with a shoulder of lamb and smoked paprika.* The shutter clicks.

1. The wooden spice box is a motif. It appears and reappears at formative and pivotal moments in the characters' lives. It contains Mariam's hidden letters, but why else is it important?

2. Gabriel could be described as a bitter old man, resentful of his fate and outwardly rude to Jennifer, Harry's parents, and several others. But he has many redeeming qualities, including an inadvertent wit. What evidence does the book provide that Gabriel is actually a romantic at heart and has a softer side?

3. Food. There's plenty of it in the novel, including references to aubergines, paprika, garlic, baked lamb, and many other traditional Armenian dishes and delicacies. Why do you think food is frequently referred to in the book? Why are mealtimes cherished by the characters? How important is food as a cultural identifier? Discuss your own culinary heritage and food traditions and their significance (if any) in your life.

4. At the start of the novel, Gabriel tells Mariam a folktale about a man who was taken by the Grim Reaper on the day of his wedding. Later, in the wilds, following their expulsion from Eastern Turkey, he relates the story of the Seven Stars. What purpose do Armenian folktales serve within the framework of the novel? How do they connect the characters to their past and foreshadow events?

5. There was a thriving asbestos mine in the Troodos mountains of Cyprus where thousands of Armenian refugees worked, including Gabriel. He had a love-hate relationship with the mine. In the novel, how is the mine portrayed as both a positive and negative force in Gabriel's life and for the mining community as a whole?

THOMAS DUNNE BOOKS

St. Martin's Press

6. Gabriel is a stickler for tradition, dead set against his granddaughter marrying a non-Armenian. Why is he (and his friend Partogh) so opposed to intermarriage? Discuss the reasons. Is there any justification for his stubbornness?

7. Why did Mariam's mother dress her as a boy when the family were marched from their homes, and why did this unwittingly lead to their separation?

8. Katerina and Ara come from different worlds, England and Cyprus, but they are intrinsically linked by their ancestral past. How does Katerina's growing awareness of her family history help her to grow as a person? To what extent do you feel people are shaped by their past and even their ancestral history?

9. The pocket watch is final proof for Gabriel that Katerina is his great-niece. Why is the watch so important to the family? Discuss its physical and metaphorical significance.

10. Many Armenians fled their homes in 1915 clutching only family pictures. Why was photography a fitting profession for Gabriel, and what role do photographs play in the novel?

11. "The café was popular with Turks and Armenians, many of whom were close friends. We were used to living together, comfortable companions in spite of our history." What made the Turks and Armenians of Cyprus comfortable companions? Why was Gabriel particularly fond of his Turkish neighbor Begum?